NEW YORK TIMES & USA TODAY BESTSELLING AUTHOR

NICOLE BLANCHARD

DEDICATION

To the Beauty & the Beast lovers who preferred the beast

CONTENTS

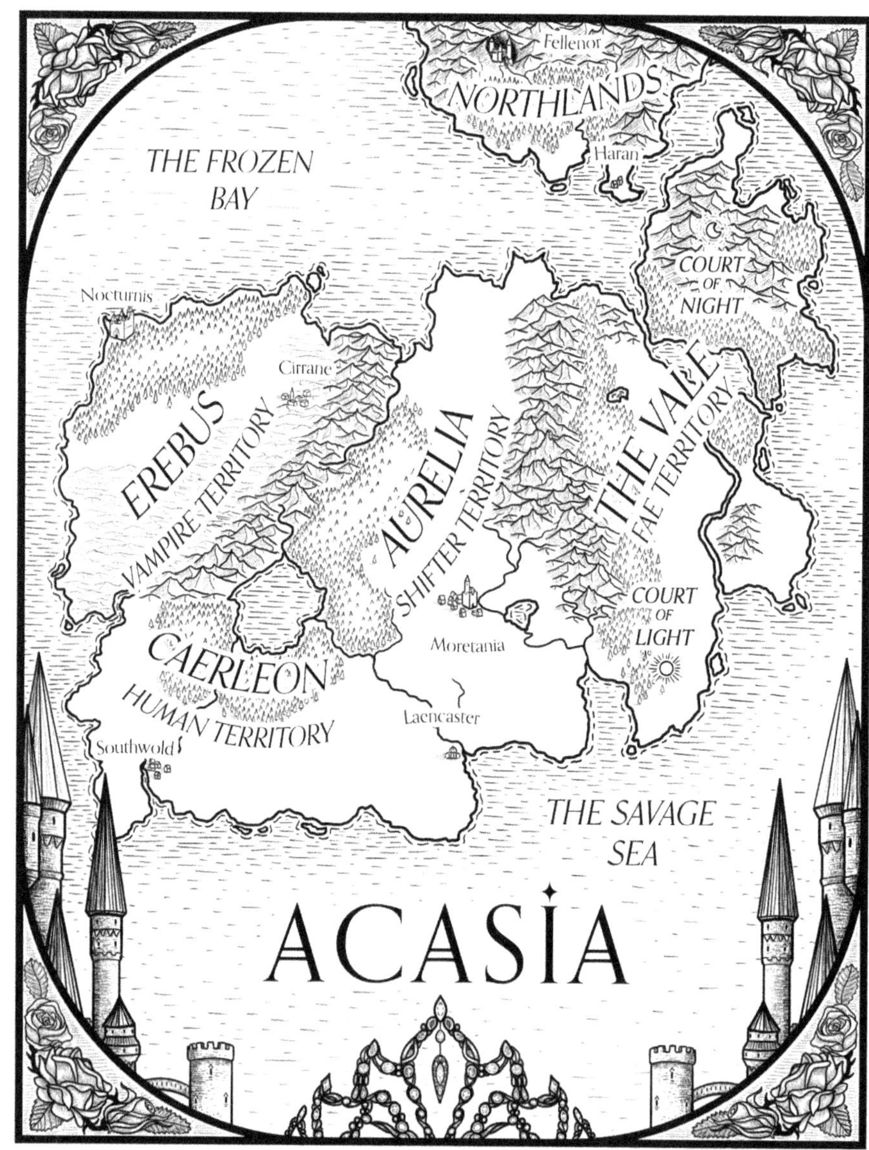
Fellenor
NORTHLANDS
Haran
THE FROZEN
BAY
COURT
OF
NIGHT
Nocturnis
Cirrane
EREBUS
VAMPIRE TERRITORY
AURELIA
SHIFTER TERRITORY
THE VALE
FAE TERRITORY
COURT
OF
LIGHT
Moretania
CAERLEON
HUMAN TERRITORY
Laencaster
Southwold
THE SAVAGE
SEA
ACASIA

ELENA

The sight of blood before breakfast was never a pleasant start to the day.

"Hold still you damned ingrate," I hissed under my breath. When the farmer rolled away from the needle and thread I was using to stitch up his wound, I ordered the attending novices to take his shoulders and legs to keep him from moving. It was nearing sunrise, and blood soaked from neck to ankle in a crimson wash. I had seconds, maybe less, before the life under my hands slipped through it.

"Don't let him move," I warned them, as I bent over the battered body in front of me.

"Curse ye', stupid bleedin' wench," the farmer muttered through gritted teeth. He was on the edge of death, but had strength enough to make scathing remarks.

I paid the novices shocked reactions as much mind as I did the farmer's vulgar cursing, which was none. The moment I'd received the call of an injured tenant, I'd slipped out of bed and into the black robes provided by the priests, as I'd done every morning since I arrived at the temple under the cover of night. The sky was dreary when I found them in the bowels of the surgery with the bleeding human farmer moaning and ashen on the table before me.

As I threaded the needle, peace stole over me, steadying my hands and clearing my mind of intrusive thoughts. I gave my assistants one last stern look to remind them to keep him as still as possible, then I went to work. With the bit of mangled flesh pinched between my forefingers, I began the long, arduous work of joining the ragged edges of the wound with care and precision. It was an intricate, tedious task, but as it often did, it soothed my riotous thoughts. Save for a whine here and a jerk there, the farmer contained his responses to the pain as I repaired the damage.

By the time I tended the wound to my exacting satisfaction, he'd given into the pain and surrendered to unconsciousness. His slack face and bone white complexion made him look like a corpse. It gave me a jolt to see his ashen face slack when it was full with such life and rage moments ago. The fragility of human life stole my breath. How easy a life was to lose—and how powerful to restore it.

"Just resting, milady," said one of the novices under her breath.

I shook my head as a chilled calm steadied my voice and resolve. "He'll need it," I replied, taking the proffered towels damp with an astringent cleaning solution for my bloodied hands. The farmer's waiting family stepped forward from where they'd been waiting in an alcove. To them, I said, "He will be just fine. He must rest here for a few more days so we can check him for fever. Once he's cleared, you'll be able to take him home."

A woman, his wife I assumed, stepped forward and laid a hand on my shoulder. "I can't thank you enough for your kindness, your highness. Acasia is blessed to have you," she said.

A shock reverberated throughout me. It had been a long time since anyone had addressed me by my royal title. Even longer since I'd thought of it. An icy apprehension crept over me, numbing my previously nimble fingers which were chilled from the still-drying solution. A shiver threatened at the base of my spine, but I refused to let it come to fruition and instead straightened it in defiance. The woman, clueless to my internal struggle, squeezed my shoulder, and I remembered to smile and thank her.

After she left, I dried my hands on a clean towel and turned to my assistants. "You may move him to the recovery beds to rest. Please inform me if he shows any symptoms of fever."

"Yes, my lady," they said in unison. One of them signaled for a waiting male who strode in, head bowed, and scooped up the patient to take him to the attached surgery. The novices filed out after them, leaving me alone and surrounded by a bloody mess.

Idleness had never been one of my strong suits, and although I wasn't required to clean up after each patient, I couldn't sit still long enough to let the mess go untouched. If a novice found me, I'd no doubt be berated for doing chores unbefitting of my station. A princess, they'd gasp, should not be cleaning, as though it were an atrocity. There were males for that chore. I snorted as I tossed the soiled towels into a bin and began wiping the stone table with a clean one. A princess shouldn't be hiding in a temple, either.

A princess should rule, my brother often reminded me in his letters.

I pushed the thought of him to the back of my mind and focused on the task at hand. My growling stomach that drew me away from cleaning, and to the kitchens, in search of breakfast before my regular daily visits from the ailing began.

The temple in the morning, before its inhabitants

woke, was my favorite part of the day. Cook and his helpers were the only ones awake, and the halls were quiet and smelled of fresh baked bread with a dash of cinnamon. Until patients started arriving and the other novices woke to tend to their duties, I'd be blessedly alone with only my food for company.

After retrieving a tray of bread and fruit rations from the cook, I excused myself to the gardens where no one would disturb me. The surgery had been my domain since the day I arrived at the temple. The healer at the time didn't want an apprentice, especially a disgraced princess. Unlike life at the castle, they required every person at the temple to pull their own weight. I was used to giving orders, not taking them. It took her death last spring and the subsequent overwhelming responsibilities of the lives in my hands for me to realize why she'd been so strict. The first time I lost a life, I'd gone to her grave and wept.

If the nobility could see me now, they wouldn't recognize me. I wore a plain wool gown, ate tasteless meals, and worked for my keep. Men's work, they'd say with a sniff and an upturned nose. I used to think the same, until they banished me to the temple, though they wouldn't call it that. A respite, the advisors had said, until they figured out what to do with me.

As I stuffed myself with raisin bread drizzled with honey, I wondered if it would be possible for me to never return. I could live my life out in peace here at the temple. No more political machinations or backhandedness. Saving lives was tough work, but unlike being a princess it was honest, fulfilling work.

When I cleaned my plate, I gave it to a servant waiting in the hall to do my rounds in the garden. Besides tending to the sick and the injured, I maintained the temple's store of herbs and medicines in the attached courtyards. I checked the seedlings I planted recently, pruned those with overgrowth, and gathered any supplies I was running low on in the baskets stacked in a corner. By the time I finished, the sun had risen over the tops of the stone enclosure. I warmed myself for a moment in the radiant heat, my face upturned, before beginning the busiest part of my day.

I opened my eyes, blinded at first by the brilliant light, and found I wasn't alone as I'd assumed.

"Sister," the figure said, and for a moment I thought I was imagining the image of my brother.

But it couldn't be.

He looked wholly unlike the older brother I'd left behind those years ago. Even if it was just a dream, I drank in the sight of him, hope fluttering in my chest like a baby bird ready to take wing for the first time. I'd missed him so much. He was the only family I had left in this world.

As he drew closer, I studied how much he'd changed.

There was a harshness about his face that wasn't there the last time I'd seen him, more than three years before. Silver threaded through the gilt color of his hair, and deep grooves carved into the corners of his mouth and along his brow. It was as though he'd aged a dozen years in the time since I'd seen him, and I ached at the lost time, the reunion bittersweet.

"Brother," I managed, my voice faint, before he tugged me forward and into his arms.

He wasn't a figment of my imagination.

"Elena," he said into my hair. "It has been much too long."

I buried my nose into the coarse material of his overcoat and inhaled the familiar scent of spices and tobacco from his favored pipes. Emotion long buried clawed at my throat, stung my eyes. I was grateful my hands were full because I would have been tempted to throw them around his shoulders and such a show of emotion would have embarrassed us both, even though we were alone. A display of that sort would have been frowned upon in public. Blatant displays of affection were characterized as masculine. Calm, cool reasoning was favored in Acasian society, even out here in the rural area where the temple was located.

"What are you doing here?" I asked when he released me, and I was certain I had my response tightly lidded. "Has something happened?"

The once familiar gaze studied me without revealing anything. As a result of constant scrutiny, Gideon had always been much more adept at controlling himself than I had been. Reserved. Composed. It made him favored among the court in the capital. "It would be best if we could speak inside," he said.

Not for the first time, I wish I had a modicum of his self-control. He should have been king, though it was unheard of for the crown to be passed to a male descendant. If he had, he wouldn't have embarrassed our people as I had. "I need to take these to the surgery and then I can meet you in my rooms."

"As you wish," he said, and then bowed as I hurried away.

"I'll just be a moment," I assured him. I wanted to reach out, touch his arm to make sure he was real again, but for once, I controlled my impulses.

Nerves warred in my stomach as I hurried to the surgery, but I didn't let them show in my expression. I'd managed the last three years without betraying my feelings to the curious faces around me and I wasn't going to allow it now. Gideon wasn't the only one who'd changed. I shouldered through the door and was met with the startled gaze of a novice attending to one of my regular patients.

"Leisha," I said with a nod.

"Milady," she replied.

"Would you mind taking over the surgery for a short time? I have some business to attend to."

Leisha has been with me since the first night I arrived at the temple, battered, beaten down, and a shadow of the person I'd once been. She stood by my side in the surgery during the most difficult procedures. I could confide in her and for a moment, I considered it, but I decided to see what Gideon had to say first.

If she was shocked, she didn't let it show. "Of course, my lady."

"Thank you." She went back to attending the patient, and I put away the herbs and tidied them. When I couldn't put it off any longer, I added, "Send for me if you get too busy."

"Yes, my lady," she answered.

I found Gideon waiting inside my sparse living quarters. I'd long since gotten used to the lack of ornamentation, but based on his reaction, he was still quite used to the lavishness of the castle in the capital city of Aurelia. My quarters were identical to any of the other novices at the temple: a simple bedroom with an attached washroom and a small fireplace to keep warm. I kept so busy, the only reason I was even in my room was to sleep and dress, otherwise I was at the surgery or working in the garden.

"You said you have news?" I asked without preamble.

"I do, though it won't be news you'll like." His deep

frown emphasized the extra lines in his face, and it reminded me of the elderly farmer I'd stitched together not hours ago. The farmer had been worn tough from many years under the sun, from hard labor and fighting for survival. Maybe it wasn't so different for my brother, who'd had to weather court politics and societal pressures in my absence.

I forced out a breath and scooped back my unruly dark curls that had escaped from their plait. "Well, out with it then," I said.

"You know as well as I, the time to return to Aurelia grows closer."

If I'd been less trained, if I hadn't spent years of my own facing those same courts, my knees would have buckled. "I'm well aware, however I thought circumstances being what they are, our cousin, the queen-regent would take my place." I said without a betraying tremor.

"It appears the deal our father made with The Dragon still holds. He wants you."

I turned away and used the pretense of preparing tea as an excuse to hide how much his news affected me. "Oh?"

"Seleste made it clear about your—difficulties. She even offered him a place as king by her side, but he refused. Told her he has more money than the Goddess herself, why would he want to be king?"

"I bet she took that well," I said. "I thought she was

marrying a lord from the Ursine clan. Lord Blaque hasn't found a mate? I would have thought he'd find someone to mate." My voice sounded breathless, hopeful, even to my ears. Foolish girl. My desperate plea since they had sent me to the temple was the hope—the wish—that my failures had also been my saving grace. That the dragon I'd been promised to as an infant had learned of my failures and decided not to have me as a mate after all.

My brother, who'd been so easy to smile when we were young, remained stone-faced. "No one else would have him."

"Lucky me," I said.

"This is your chance, Elena," Gideon said, after a long silence.

My hands began to sweat, and I wiped them on my serviceable apron. For a moment, I yearned for the finery that came with being a future queen. It was easy to hide behind the dresses and accoutrements, the glittering jewelry and elaborate coifs. "What do you mean?"

If possible, Gideon's face hardened even more. "Your chance to undo the disgrace of losing the throne. It's not as though you have a choice."

At his words, my hands fisted in my skirts, the nails digging into the fleshy parts of my palm, but I couldn't feel their bite. I'd gone numb. "I beg your pardon?"

Gideon eyes flashed in annoyance, but I was used to his quick temper. He may be composed most of the time, but it didn't always outdo his natural character. Like most other males, it was hard for him to see logic, reason. I'd been compelled to follow his directives when I was younger, but I'd come into my own in the years since he secreted me from the castle. I wouldn't follow him blindly, no matter his reasoning or the difference in our age. "Lord Blaque expects you at the castle within a week's time to take your place as his mate. You've known this was coming, even if you can't shift, you're still of royal blood," he added in a low voice.

It had been years, but the part of me bruised by my failure still ached. "Thank you for reminding me," I said. He sighed and even if I wasn't gifted with the power of empathy, I sensed the waves of frustration emanating from him. "Is there nothing else that can be done?"

"Elena, don't be stubborn about this. If we back out of the contract, it would be devastating for Acasia."

That he would bring this up today when my longing for the capital and the castle was so strong wasn't fair. I turned away from him to give myself time to think, without the pleading look on his face swaying my decision. My mind raced, which caused me to pace. Since they had sequestered me in the temple, I'd learned to be patient and consider my words before speaking. But I didn't want to be patient or thoughtful now. As much as I loved the temple and my work, it wasn't home like the castle.

"Gideon," I winced at the pleading tone in my voice.

He sighed without meeting my eyes. "This isn't only about The Dragon, Sister, or the crown. It's about Father." There was a pregnant pause until he continued, "He's dying."

2

RHYSANDER

Old as the land itself and once teaming with magick as ancient as the stone, the mountain that surrounded the Northlands had been home to the Dragon-Clan for as far back as Immortals could recall.

My father used to rattle about the endless crypts, plumbing their depths and spinning tales about our ancestors until he joined them many years ago, when I was still new to my wings. His spirit still lingered and as I've gotten older, I retraced his steps, though much has changed since he was alive.

The constant drip of moisture from the ice river above kept me company as I wandered down the twists and turns. I could sense the loss of magick, of life. It's as though the heart of the mountain, the stronghold of the Dragon-Clan, was ceasing to beat.

I reached out a claw to trace the etchings in the stone walls that were worn soft with time. The drawings depicted different scenes from our history, the rise and fall of the Dragon-Clan—still the most powerful shifters in all of Acasia—but certainly not as strong in numbers as we were in days of old.

"You spend too much time in these crypts, my friend," came a familiar voice.

I looked over my shoulder to find Alaric studying an etching of a dragon egg hatching from a bed of roses. "Better here than up there," I answered. "Besides, I'm not the only one shirking my duties."

Alaric merely smiled serenely. What was it about the Fae that made them seem so aloof and mischievous at the same time? "We readied the carriages. Are you sure you don't want me to go with you? Traveling alone in this climate is dangerous. Even for the mighty Lord of Dragons."

I allowed him to guide me through the passages back to the surface. Alaric knew the crypts almost as well as I did, though it wasn't because he was raised here, it was because his Fae senses were more sensitive than my own. "I've more use for you here while I'm away. The humans are growing more and more restless, and I fear another attack is forthcoming. I'd rather travel with a small group of my best soldiers with you here to supervise."

Alaric studied me in the dim candlelight of the castle

foyer. The sun shone in the Northlands most of the day, but it was almost always from behind a cover of dull, gray clouds. "You don't want to take your time with your new bride? It will be your wedding night after all. Perhaps I should send along a gift."

I snorted as I dressed in a heavy cape and fastened the buckles on my dragonhide boots. "The last thing I want is to spend more time with the girl than I have to. I'll fetch her from the castle, let the priests perform the binding ceremony, mate her, then bring her home. If I'm lucky, I'll only have to see her at night thereafter to make sure she's bred successfully. And there's no way in Slaine I'd want a gift from you. The girl already has enough strings attached to her, I don't need a faerie bargain along with it."

"If you think any woman would be happy with that arrangement, I think you're sorely mistaken," Alaric said, ignoring my dig. "Shifters are a feisty breed and their women are the worst of the lot. Giving orders and disparaging their males." He shook his head. "I don't know how you do it. You're a glutton for punishment."

I didn't answer as we headed for the carriages at the front of the castle and he knew I wouldn't. I rarely talked about my first mate, and liked even less to be reminded of her. If I had a choice about the matter, I'd live the rest of my days in solitude along with the dying mountain, mating be damned.

As the Lord of the Dragon-Clan, it was my responsibility to provide for their future and part of providing was continuing the line and delivering an heir. Like the rest of the shifters in Acasia, the Dragon-Clansmen had suffered from reduced numbers over the past few centuries, so continuing the line is even more imperative than ever.

It's why I agreed to the arrangement with King Baron twenty years ago. In exchange for my clansmen's protection along his southern borders from the humans, he promised the hand of his firstborn daughter in return. In theory, a powerful shifter should be strong enough to carry a dragonborn child to term, especially if that shifter were the future queen. With most of my men at the southern border aiding the shifters in defending their lands against our restless human counterparts, we're more in need of fresh blood than ever.

Alaric stopped me as I prepared to mount my horse. Normally, I would have flown to the capital in my shifted form, but my future mate would need the carriages that followed me for the return trip.

"You've heard the rumors, haven't you? About the princess."

Oh, I'd heard rumors.

That Elena of the Avian-Clan was more beautiful than the sunrise. That before she'd been disgraced, it had been foretold she'd be the most powerful queen of the age, even more powerful than her mother, who had been a rare shifter indeed. It's why she they cast from the castle when she couldn't shift. Cursed, they said.

But who wasn't cursed in this world, in one way or another?

I lifted a brow. "I've heard the rumors, but I would prefer to observe them for myself." My tone brooked no argument. Naturally, Alaric took no notice.

"Her cousin, the queen-regent, another Avian-Clan named Seleste. Wouldn't she suit better? Certainly, she'd be a more powerful alliance than the princess."

Mounting the horse, which snorted underneath me, I gathered the reins in my hand and sent Alaric a quelling look. "I have more power than I need, and the queen-regent is much too… enthusiastic for my tastes."

No, the princess would suit my needs nicely. If nothing else, her disgrace from the throne should make her more biddable, I hoped. The last thing I needed was another strong-willed, demanding female to share my bed. There were quite enough of those already.

I waved to the gathering of Dragon-Clan members from the village and servants pouring from the castle to see me off.

"If you're counting on this girl to be as docile as you're imagining, I have a feeling you will be disappointed," Alaric said. "What if she turns out to be your true mate?"

At that, I laughed. "I have no interest in anything other than an heir. As long as she's pregnant within the year, I won't be disappointed. Besides, no shifter, even a princess, is a match for my dragon."

I made no mention of true mates—such a thing was legend among our people. A faerie tale to encourage children to make favorable matches or what adolescent girls told themselves to make marrying an ancient match more attractive. True mates were a thing of lore—Immortal mates who would bring Acasia back from damnation.

My horse snorted, and I patted his shoulder. "Indeed," I murmured.

SEVEN INTERMINABLE NIGHTS passed since I departed from my beloved mountains in Fellenor, the Northlands' capital city. A small regiment of men accompanied me across the Northlands at a breakneck pace where we boarded a ship in the tiny village of Haran on the coast. Crossing the Frozen Bay had been arduous and required long hours in my shifted form, breathing fire at the glaciers that blocked our path. I would melt them and they'd freeze as soon as the ship was through.

By the time we reached the Corinthine Woods just

north of the capital city of Aurelia, frost coated the furs worn by most of the regiment. A vicious blizzard blotted out all sight when we disembarked from the ship, but I could tell the moment I set foot to frost that something was wrong. The port village of Braedon was little more than a shantytown, a stop for travelers on their way to the Northlands. Despite this, it was too quiet, too still. Though the village was small, the times I've traveled to and from the Northlands, it bustled with life.

The only sound came from the howling of the wind as it whipped through our furs and capes. The swirling snow hampered visibility to mere feet in front of us.

"Do you smell that?" my lieutenant, Adriel, asked. At his words, the others in our small group scented the air.

I lifted my head to the wind, my nostrils flaring as I pulled in a deep breath. An acrid taste bathed the back of my throat and coated my tongue. A familiar taste. Ash and ember and brimstone.

"Fire," Adriel breathed. "There's a fire close."

Drawing my weapon, I motioned the others behind me. The scent of burning wood and blistering leather grew stronger as we pierced the blizzard's lacy arms in the direction of town. Soon, the white flurries became tinged with gray soot, dancing along with the pristine flakes. It smeared on our faces and coated our boots and furs in a thick layer of grime. Adriel was the first to reach the outer edges of Braedon. What he saw brought him up short.

The village, what was left of it, was a smoldering ruin. Tendrils of black smoke curled up from what remained of the wooden buildings and mixed with the falling snow, turning the ground at our feet to soiled slush. It was eerily quiet. Not even the animals in the nearby forest made a sound.

We moved in closer, silent as the shadows, and I shifted into my half-Dragon form. Scales erupted in patches over my body, up my throat and down my arms, providing both armor against potential attack and protection against the elements, as I shed my furs and cloak to make it easier to maneuver through the wreckage. My harsh exhalations turned to steam and my eyes became glazed, focused, allowing me to view our surroundings at a level so minuscule I could see each spark from the embers in a nearby fire in acute detail.

My voice, when I spoke, was a deeper rumble. "Stay on guard," I ordered. "Whoever set these fires could still be close."

I circled around the perimeter as my men ventured farther into the village to investigate. There were fresh tracks leading south from the village on the road toward the capital. Whoever had attacked had left on foot, human foot. If it had been a shifter, they would have used their shifted form to make a faster getaway. Tooth and claw and wing were far more effective than human flesh and bone.

Adriel had reached the same conclusion. "I've never seen humans attack this far north. They've grown bold. Too bold."

I gnashed my fangs. The people of Braedon were distant members of the Dragon-Clan, those who could not stomach the blustery Northlands winters, but wanted to be near their home—or the one they used to have before it all went to Slaine. They were supposed to be able to rely on me for protection and I'd failed them. Again. Not only were they suffering from the curse intended for me, but it cost them their lives.

If I had any doubts about following through with the deal I'd made with the Darkmoores, this attack had erad- icated them. I'd mate the damn girl, and exact my revenge on those responsible for killing my people when the time was right.

They'd regret the day they crossed the Dragon-Clan.

I'd make sure of it.

3

ELENA

The journey back to the home I never thought I'd see again was miserable. A wintry wind fought us every step of the way. It didn't escape my notice that I could consider the perilous journey an omen. The Goddess wouldn't be the only one displeased by my return.

If Gideon had any misgivings, he didn't tell me, preferring to keep to his own carriage when he wasn't overhead in his shifted form as a proud hawk. The distance between us didn't help my growing dread. When we were younger, he'd often shift when it was just the two of us and fly overhead for hours while I raced through the nearby woods. His loud birdcall would nip at my heels and I would fill the trees with my shrieks of laughter. He had never made me believe I was less of a person because I couldn't shift.

There was no laughter now, no carefree exploring. Gideon had become stoic in my absence, resolute, and it showed. Stoicism was revered in Acasia, especially in men, and I knew Gideon did what he could in the years since I've been gone to fight tooth and claw out of our father's hotheaded shadow. I glanced through the frosted window of my carriage and found him just above our line of guards. His flight hadn't wavered since we set off on the last, most brutal leg of our journey.

A part of me couldn't help but wonder if he stayed in shifted form on purpose so he wouldn't have to socialize with me. I wouldn't blame him, not really. I'd let more than just myself down when it became common knowledge that I was declared unfit for the throne. Now, the only value I could provide was my body, and how it could service the infamously deadly Lord of the Dragon-Clan.

The thought of facing the castle, the court, and the advisors—who'd deemed me inferior—sent a trail of shivers dancing down my spine, as menacing as a knot of poisonous spiders. I pulled the fur wrap more securely around my shoulders and gave myself a shake. I'd faced far worse circumstances than their disapproving stares, though I couldn't think of any if pressed. The overwhelming defeat I wore like a chain around my neck only seemed to grow heavier the closer we got to the castle.

I had no illusions about my reception. No one in Acasia wanted me to darken the court halls again. I was an embarrassment, a warning to children who didn't do their chores. I'd become a cautionary tale in the time since I left the palace. "This is what happens when you disobey the Goddess' wishes," they'd say. Her mother shirked her duties and married a warrior, a brute, so the Goddess burdened her with a shiftless daughter. A male child would have been more acceptable than a girl who couldn't shift into her gifted form. And most women were looked down upon if they birthed only males. If my birth hadn't killed her, my failure would have.

"Are you well, your highness?" Leisha asked quietly from the opposite side of the carriage.

"I will be," I replied with what I hoped was a serene smile. "I'm unused to traveling so much, I'm afraid. It makes one miss the temple."

"Begging your pardon, my lady, but you're not excited to see the castle again?"

I peered back out the frosted window, unable to repress the foreboding shiver that stole down the neck of my dress and danced along my spine. I could see the barest hint of shadow from its dominating presence on the horizon. I was excited to spend time with my brother, that much was true, but the castle? No. I was dreading the moment I stepped foot inside the ancient cobbled halls and faced the reality that had me stealing away in the middle of the night, shame nipping at my heels.

"I'M READY," I said to Gideon.

He shouldered through the door without another word, and then there was no going back. A flurry of movement greeted me, and I wondered if I was the only person who wasn't aware of the sudden change in plans. Priests were scuttling back and forth with tapestries and ancient, dusty tomes. Gideon dropped my hand to converse with them, and a trio of servants rushed forward at once to pull me into the whirlwind.

They etched symbols into the wood floor at my feet and wrenched my gown from my body, replacing with a fresh one. No one gave a thought to modesty—not that it mattered. They were so consumed by their tasks that no one noticed as I dressed. Besides, they considered my body a thing these days. An idol. I'd ceased to be simply a girl. I was to become a queen. Gideon and the oldest of the priests huddled together, deep in conversation. They placed a crown on my head and then a disembodied hand pushed me forward.

Everyone turned to face me as I stepped into the circle in the center of the room, and it was in that moment my nerves returned in full. Incense choked all breathable air from my surroundings and I sucked it in with great heaves, but it didn't calm my racing heart. I wondered if they laced the incense with something, a drug, maybe, but I didn't have time to consider it more before the priests were surrounding me. Perhaps my reaction wasn't because of the concoction. It was possible the sheer swiftness of activity had caused my head to spin.

I sought Gideon's eyes over the bowed heads and flowing robes, but it was too dark for me to see. The candlelight only showed as far as the edge of the circle. Beyond that was nothingness.

"Your hand, Princess," said the priest in front of me, who had just spoken with Gideon.

It trembled, but only slightly, as I placed it in the priest's grasp. He lifted a dagger and though I knew he wasn't going to hurt me, a flash of apprehension stole through me at the sight of the wickedly sharp blade. The priestess next to him lifted a weighty chalice and brought it underneath my hand. With one flick of his wrist, the priest sliced open a thin line on the meat of my palm, causing me to gasp. Blood pooled out of the wound and then dripped in a steady stream down my palm and into the chalice.

The priestess took the chalice as the priests circled around me began to chant. The scent of the incense grew stronger, and with it, so did the sense of trepidation writhing around in my stomach. Sweat beaded up on my forehead and it felt as though I were floating above my body, looking down at the ceremony below. The priestess was mixing herbs and tonics in the chalice, though I didn't have a clue what they were. Such magick has been passed from mother to daughter down the Druid line for centuries.

I'd been told as long as I could remember the ceremony was an honor. My mother should have been the one to prepare me, teach me, but her untimely death had stolen that opportunity.

Now, I was to face it alone.

"Take the chalice and drink," the priest in front of me said as he retrieved it from the priestess.

I wanted to glance at Gideon for reassurance, but I could only stare at the concoction I was supposed to imbibe. It looked awful and smelled worse. As I brought it to my lips, my knees wanted to buckle beneath me and my stomach gave a great heave, but I locked my legs and swallowed. I'd made enough mistakes. Showing myself to be a fool in front of the most respected members of the court would not be one of them.

Resolved, I tossed back the rancid-smelling liquid and forced myself to drink down every drop. When I finished, someone took the chalice from my hand and the surrounding chanting grew louder.

For a moment, I wondered why no one in the castle

could hear it, and then a horrible, searing pain overtook me. No amount of willpower could keep me from falling to my knees or silence the scream that tore from my throat. It felt like someone was rearranging my bones from the inside out. I heard a scuffling sound and then harsh whispers, and then I couldn't focus on anything but trying to keep my bones in their correct places.

I didn't know how long it went on, but it felt like an eternity. The thick incense and the pressing darkness consumed me along with the unrelenting pain. Minutes, then hours, passed, and I knew something was wrong.

I wasn't shifting.

"Gideon," I whispered, though to the knives of pain in my head, it felt like a scream. "Gideon, something's wrong."

Liquid fire burst through my chest and I swallowed back another scream. I didn't want to seem weak, didn't want them to think their queen couldn't handle shifting like every other person in the realm, even though I was certain I was being torn in two.

"Elena," came Gideon's voice. "Elena, all you have to do is let go. Let go and the pain will go away."

I tried. Goddess above, I tried. No matter how much I tried to relax, how hard I breathed through the agony, there was no relief, no shift to take it away. "I can't," I moaned, after an eternity. "Something's wrong, Gideon. I can't shift."

His silence was answer enough. Even the chanting seemed to hush at my words.

"*Come, now,*" *the priest said, at last.* "*You must do this for Acasia.*"

In that moment, had I access to a weapon, I would have gladly sunk it in his smug face. Such a violent outburst wasn't befitting of a woman, so I dropped my gaze. Sweat dripped from my brow onto the wooden floor beneath me. It coated my new dress and made it cling to my skin. "*I'm trying,*" *I seethed.* "*Something is wrong. It's not working.*"

A fracture furrowed its way through the very center of me and I knew if I let it go on much longer it would break me completely. "*Make it stop. Make it stop,*" *I shouted.*

Gideon barked at the priest who nodded to the priestess. An acrid scent filled the air and then someone grabbed my arm and cut another slice through my palm. The metallic odor mixed with the brew, and then someone shoved it under my nose. It smelled even worse the second time around, but I didn't care. I'd drink whatever they wanted if it would take the pain away.

It went down my throat like rivulets of ice, cooling and numbing everything in its wake. The pain subsided in gradual waves until it left me exhausted and cold on the floor, surrounded by concerned and mistrustful faces.

Gideon shouldered his way through them and fell to his knees. He gathered me up in his arms like he used to when we were kids, but the look on his face was anything but affectionate.

"*What does this mean?*" *I asked him.*

"It means we must get you out of the castle," was his grim reply.

"My lady?" A tentative hand on my shoulder ripped me from the foggy reverie. "We're here."

An icy sweat dampened my brow and the meager contents of my stomach threatened to reappear. Leisha offered a cloth soaked in lavender mist to wash my face. Appearing at court for the first time in years with a sour sweat streaming from my pores would be a fatal mistake —one I couldn't afford. The restorative soothed my nerves and left a refreshing, pleasant floral note on my skin to mask any apprehension. Living amongst the humans at the temple had given me more of a reprieve than I'd thought.

The shifter race, gifted with enhanced senses and keen eyesight in addition to their inherited familial powers, wouldn't hesitate to go for my proverbial—and literal—throat at the first sign of weakness. I had no illusions about meeting the Dragon. Revered as the fiercest of all our kind, he would be no different than all the rest. In fact, it wouldn't surprise me if he were worse. The rumors I'd heard—

"Is something wrong?" Leisha inquired.

I gathered my furs around my throat and accepted the hand of the waiting steward. Lord Blaque was the least of my worries. First, I wanted to face the court and see my father. The Dragon couldn't be worse than that.

Could he?

"All is well," I told her, pleased my voice didn't waver.

Maybe saying it aloud would make it true.

"Should I walk with you to your rooms to get freshened up?" she asked. Her eyes were tight with concern.

I shook my head. "I'd like to visit my father straightaway."

"But isn't Lord Blaque going to be waiting for you?"

"I will visit my father first," I reiterated.

Leisha bowed her head, but it wasn't fast enough to hide the look of reprimand on her face. "Yes, my lady."

Gideon disappeared, no doubt to announce our arrival, and I would take advantage of the opportunity to slip away, despite the disapproval I'd receive as a result. I would not shirk my duties, but my priority was seeing my father before it was too late.

The first steward I found dressed in simple breeches and a clean linen shirt gaped at me as I asked him where the King was resting. He pointed toward a section of the castle used for treating the ill and injured, and I hastened toward it before he could ask what the disgraced princess was doing back in the castle.

A wave of sour air greeted me upon entrance to my

father's chambers. I pasted a smile on my face that I hoped didn't look as brittle as it felt, even though there was no one to see it. His room was empty save for his wheezing form, a shadow of the man he'd once been. I turned from the thought and the wave of sadness that crested in my chest and strode to the enormous windows across from his bed. The ancient shutters creaked in protest as I shoved them open. The healer would no doubt have my hide, but I didn't care. I didn't have it in me to let my father, the greatest man I'd ever known, waste away in his own filth. It couldn't be healthy to stew in the scent of sickness.

I crossed to his bed, resting a hip on the chair arm next to him as I studied his recumbent form. It wasn't supposed to be like this. A rogue tear streaked down my cheek, and I wiped it away with a violent movement.

My father, much as shifter-kind would like to disagree, was a great man. Despite the temper so looked down upon amongst our kind, he had been a caring person and he absolutely doted on my mother. According to the best healer the lands could provide, his illness resulted from heartbreak after my mother died giving birth to me. As I smoothed his chestnut hair away from his brow, I chided myself for talking of him in the past tense. Gideon may think he would die, but I wasn't so certain. Or maybe I was deluded. Even so, I'd rather be delusional for a while longer than give up on him forever. I'd already lost one parent…I couldn't bear to lose another.

"He was asking for you," Gideon said, entering from Father's adjoining study. He didn't join me by his bedside. Instead, he hovered in the doorway. "I knew I'd find you here. The pain became too much, so I instructed the healer to supply him with a sleeping draught."

I turned away from him, my throat closing around the bitter words that threatened to spew forth. I knew there wouldn't be a joyous conversation to be had at our parting, but I, at the very least, wanted to tell him good-bye. To have him call me La-lena one last time like he did when Gideon and I were children. The sickness caused by losing a mate, when the match was said to be blessed by the Goddess, was enough to cause one of the greatest men I'd ever known to whither away to nothing.

"I'm sorry, sister," Gideon offered, but the words sounded hollow.

"No, don't be silly," I said, though I didn't know if I was talking to Gideon…or myself. "He needs his rest." I shifted enough to brush back a lock of hair from Father's brow, frowning when I caught sight of all the silver strands. He'd been so vital once, so solid. "Do the healers bring any news about his condition? Have there been any improvements?" I looked back knowing I was grasping at nothing, but trying anyway. I would always keep trying.

To lose hope was to give up, and I would be damned if I was going to do either.

Gideon winced and I took that like a stake to the heart. I forced a smile anyway. "No matter. I'm sure by the time I'm able to visit next, he'll be up and about ordering everyone around again." But I'd been saying that for years. The illness had given us only a brief time with him. I'd been but a young girl when he took to bed and never got up… unless it was to babble.

"Elena," Gideon began, a spiel I'd heard more times than I could count, "I don't want you to be disappointed."

His fierce expression, so different from the composed mask I'd grown used to him wearing during our travels, reminded me so much of Father that I almost gasped aloud. They had always resembled one another. Both had broad angular jaws and deep-set eyes the color of a mountain bear's pelt.

"Then don't disappoint me," I interrupted. "There has to be something we can do to save him. Anything."

"I find it difficult to believe any magick would bring Father back from this. It would only work if Father *wanted* to live. Which I don't think you've ever really understood. He could have found another mate, continued on, but he chose not to. An Immortal without a mate is as good as having a death sentence."

Gideon's own union with a crow-shifter, from what I

could recall, had been little more than a business transaction. Their binding was cold, calculated. They were together long enough to tumble in the sheets, then kept to separate parts of the castle. I shuddered, chilled to the bone thinking about it. They'd never had children, but he'd never expressed any desire to be a father.

"We can't just let him die like this, Gideon."

But Gideon had enough; he waved a dismissive hand like I was one of the servants he ordered around. And maybe I was. For most of my life he'd been the one who raised me, gave me guidance. In some ways, he had been more a father figure than the man lying unconscious in the bed. "You're acting like a child. You cannot expect to ignore the facts in front of us. He's not getting any better. This illness has even the most skilled healers stumped. Ever since Mother died—"

I found myself on my feet, teeth bared like a lioness protecting her cub. "You act like he's already dead."

The pitying expression on Gideon's face made me wish I had tooth or claw to rip him to shreds. Shifting into a griffin would have been beneficial, or even a loon with its pointed bill would come in handy to spear Gideon until he could talk sense. "Maybe it's a good thing the Dragon is taking you to the Northlands," he said. "Evidently, the time at the temple wasn't enough to get you thinking clearly."

"Won't you consider letting him come with us?" It

was an argument we'd had years before when I'd left for Caerleon, but his responding sigh of impatience still birthed the first thread of dismay in my heart.

The thought of leaving Father was one that had kept me up at night while I was traveling back. It had been hard enough leaving him to live at the temple. Doing so now would be more permanent than I could handle. I was certain a man such as the Dragon would never entertain the thought of bringing a sickly old man all the way to the North. The cost of magick alone would be exorbitant. Our family was rich in power…but little else. The crown we wore was superficial at best, and now in my case, nonexistent.

The Dragon, however, was rumored to keep a vast horde of treasures deep within his mountains. Enough gold and riches to finance the whole of Acasia. If he had any interest in ruling our kind, he could buy and sell us out ten times over.

But no one in the capital wanted a murderer for a king. Sure, we'd bartered for his wrath to protect our borders for a time, but the ladies on the Council would rather die than have a monster like him on the throne. I bet they were certain he would be even worse than me.

"You know he isn't well enough to travel," Gideon said, interrupting my desperate thoughts. "Don't fret, sister, we have the best healers in Acasia at our disposal. They will take good care of him until it is his time."

Finally, he came to my side, pressing a kiss to my forehead. "Don't dawdle here. The Dragon is due to arrive any moment and he'll be wanting to meet you."

I managed to keep my knees locked until the door to the study clicked behind him; then I collapsed on the chair beside the bed with my face in my hands. I didn't want to leave his side, but if I didn't Gideon would be disappointed. The grief was overwhelming, but I would steal away what few moments I had left with him, Gideon—and the damned Dragon I was to mate—notwithstanding.

I swallowed down my own feelings like a bitter spoonful of medicine and leaned over my father's weakened form and whispered, "I love you," into his ear. I kissed his brow, lingering for a second to inhale his familiar scent beneath the stench of death. "I promise I'll do whatever it takes to heal you. Even mate the wretched Dragon."

4

RHYSANDER

We buried the bodies…or what remained of them.

There was nothing left of Braedon but cinders, smoke, and the ghosts of its inhabitants. It wasn't the first shifter village to be attacked of late, and I was afraid it wouldn't be the last.

My mouth tasted like ash and copper for days afterward. Death clung to my skin like an oily shadow, no matter how many times I bathed in the river that ran along the main road to Aurelia. I considered finding a caster to magick away the remains, but dismissed the idea. Like the Fae, casters were a tricky folk. Part human, part Immortal, they drew upon the magic from the land to impart simple enchantments.

But they almost always had a price.

That I knew all too well.

I tossed and turned inside my tent in an attempt to blot out the memories with sleep. But the scent of death was too strong, and my mind too weary from the days of travel. In the twilight of half-sleep, they taunted me with miseries long since gone.

Miseries that made me reconsider if mating this princess was wise after all.

I pushed up from my pallet on the frozen ground and stalked into the forest, the snow crunching underfoot. The sharp, icy bite filled my nose, erasing the scent of burnt flesh, at least momentarily. Following the sound of water trickling over rocks, I wound my way back to the river. Part of me hoped the sound could drown out my thoughts.

The conversation with Alaric had been on my mind since we left the Northlands. I didn't want another mate. If it weren't for the bargain I'd made with King Baron to protect the southern borders of Aurelia, I'd still be in my mountains, far away from these new threats against my people. Threats that were growing too close to the Northlands for my peace of mind.

I reached the river and knelt down to splash my face with the frigid water. If I couldn't sleep, then I'd keep watch over my men. The refreshing icy stream washed away the last vestiges of grogginess.

It wasn't until I was halfway through the forest to our

camp when I caught the sound over the splashing water. Feet connecting with earth. Hushed voices. The whisper of metal being drawn from a sheath.

I lifted my nose to the air and scented blood.

Human blood.

With a snarl, I shifted into my half-Dragon form and sprinted through the trees, my Immortal legs carrying me there in mere seconds.

But it was too late.

I was too late.

The humans surrounded Adriel with a knife to his throat. A slash of blood married the otherwise wholesome skin. The man at his side wielding the knife jerked his chin in my direction. Without a word, he slit Adriel's throat and a blood red smile bloomed in its wake.

An inhuman roar ripped from my throat, and wings erupted from the skin at my back. A blood-red haze covered my vision and blotted out everything but my foe.

When I was done, it was as though I'd bathed in their blood. The carnage I'd wrought surrounded me and those of my men who survived the attack watched with cautious eyes.

"Do a headcount," I ordered, my breath coming in rapid puffs as I shifted back to my human form. I didn't bother to fix my clothes or change. "Gather the dead. We bury the humans and I'll build a pyre for the others."

Without a word, they did as I bade and I carried Adriel's body myself to the pyre like we'd done with all the shifters' remains from Braedon. I shouldn't have let my thoughts consume me. I could have prevented this.

We made quick work of burying the attackers and assembling Adriel and two others onto a pyre of young pines I'd broken into tinder. With a belch of flame, the pyre caught fire. We watched until there was nothing left but ash.

The scent of charred flesh lingered on the air once more.

THE MOMENT we crossed into capital land two days later, I began counting down the seconds until we could leave again. I preferred the solace of my mountain to the hustle of the village. There were too many people. It was winter, but temperatures were sweltering compared to the Northlands.

As my irritation rose, I noticed the pointed looks the capital dwellers were sending my way. Smoke had curled from my nostrils, signaling my growing temper. The villagers gave our procession a wide berth. Either from my seething expression or the blood that still stained my clothes. I hadn't given us time to stop. We'd ridden without a break until we'd reached Aurelia.

Normally, I'd curtail my anger, but I wanted them to scurry away from me. The more they feared me, the less trouble we should have while we were in the capital. I only used violence as a last resort, but I wouldn't hesitate if threatened. I'd guarded their borders for twenty years, and I knew tales of my prowess had spread far and wide. Their fear pleased me and made it easier for me to keep my distance.

A gathering of courtiers, servants, and guardsmen clustered around the entrance to the castle. I studied their faces with disguised interest, but only recognized the Queen, Seleste. I didn't spend much time in court if I could help it, and couldn't care less about royal happenings.

I came to a stop beside the crown and dismounted. Seleste rushed to my side and offered her hand. "Lord Blaque," she greeted in a simpering voice. "So delighted to have you here at last. I hope your journey was pleasant."

She either ignored or didn't care why I was covered in blood. Perhaps she thought I ate humans for breakfast only a regular basis. "I trust my future mate made it as well."

Her eyes dimmed. "She arrived just this morning."

"I'd like to see her."

"She's busy at the moment," interjected another shifter. He stepped forward to Seleste's side and met my gaze.

"I would have thought the first item on the agenda would have been to introduce me to my mate," I told a stony-faced Gideon Darkmoore, Prince of Acasia. I recognized him after a moment from his resemblance to his father, King Baron.

"Of course, Lord Blaque," he demurred. "We'll summon her at once."

That was another reason why I hated being in the capital. The shifters in this region treated males like they were chattel to be crushed under the delicate female boot. I'd been mated to a woman like that once, and I'd be damned if I'd let anyone treat me like that again.

I'd burn in Slaine first.

My words were bitten out between gritted teeth when I spoke, "Don't bother yourself. Tell me where she is, and I'll find her."

Gideon's eyes widened a fraction in surprise. "That's unnecessary."

"I'll decide what's necessary," I replied without hesitation.

Prince Gideon's jaw tightened and for a moment I thought he would argue, but he said, "She's with our father. He's been ill since our mother passed."

"I was sorry to hear it."

Seleste snapped her fingers. "You there, show Lord Blaque to King Baron's quarters."

A maid curtsied, then said, "Yes, your highness. Right this way."

I held up a hand. Stars, these people needed help with everything, didn't they? "I can find it on my own, unless you think I need an escort."

"Of course not," Seleste said with faux cheerfulness. "You'll join us for dinner?"

Rather than argue, I agreed. "Of course."

After directing my stewards to stow my belongings in my rooms, I made my way to King Baron's quarters. The last time I was in the capital it had been to negotiate for his daughter's hand. Despite my hesitance to bind myself to another mate, I was eager to meet the princess and get it all over with so I could go back to the Northlands.

My ears picked up the sound of her voice first, not enough to make out the words, but enough to gather she was whispering encouraging sentiments to her father. She was saying her goodbyes. I couldn't decipher what she was saying, but her voice was melodious and confident, despite the grief that shadowed it.

The dragon inside my chest purred like the sound of her voice was a siren's call. It wanted her, fiercely, viciously, as it sometimes craved the blood of an enemy.

I stepped up to the door, but didn't announce myself. Dressed in a nondescript, but well-made gown and cloak, a young woman of about twenty sat at the bedside of an ailing man, her hands clasped around one of his. Her hair draped over her shoulders in a glossy length the color of burnished wood. I wanted to run my claws through it, feel it draped over my body. Because the urge to touch it was all too strong, I stepped forward and cleared my throat to call her attention.

She started, turned. A hand went to her hair, and she pushed it away from her red eyes. She'd been crying. Her cheeks were still wet from tears and the dragon snarled, wanting to lick them clean, desperate for the taste of her sorrow on my tongue.

"Are you the healer?" she asked, getting to her feet. She gestured and said, "This room, it's too stifled. My father needs fresh air. His quarters need to be cleaned more regularly, his body bathed at more frequent intervals. Just because he's dying doesn't mean he doesn't deserve to be treated with dignity. By stars, he was your King!"

I frowned at her. When was the last time someone other than Alaric had spoken to me in such a way and not been punished for it? "I'm not your healer, girl."

Her eyes flashed with a heat I felt down to the marrow. "It's *Princess*," she gritted out. "If you're not the healer, then if you'd be so kind as to fetch one, it would be most appreciated. Be quick about it, I have somewhere else I need to be soon."

It should have enraged me to have to her order me about, considering the last thing I wanted in a woman was one who had any semblance of a backbone, but I found myself stepping toward her instead of away. "There's no need," I told her.

She stepped closer to her father's slumbering form. "No need for what?"

"No need for fetching a healer. Can't you tell your father is dying? He won't have much left in this world before he ascends to the stars."

It was true. I thought it kinder not to spare her of my assessments. I could hear how frail his heart beat, the slow, death-march rattle of his lungs. He'd lost much weight since I saw him last, twenty years ago. His thick hair that had once matched the color of his daughter's, was now silver and lank. Once, he'd been a great warrior of renowned strength and power, some said he'd rivaled my own, but now his muscle had wasted away, and he looked as though one stiff wind could blow him away… if it possible for him to stand from the sick bed.

The pale skin of her face drained of all color. "How could you say such a thing? Who are you?"

"Denying it will only make it harder, Elena."

"How do you know my name?" she demanded. "Who are you?" She looked around the room as though to find someone to order me away…or escape. Then, she turned back to me. Her eyes took in my blood-stained clothes, my claws, and the steam still unfurling from my nose.

When I smiled, she took a step back, her gaze going to my fangs.

"I know your name, just as you know mine."

Her hand fluttered to her throat as she swallowed hard and met my eyes. "You're my mate," she said, her voice a whisper.

Mine, my dragon roared in response.

5

ELENA

I could wipe at my face, straighten my travel-rumpled skirts and bemoan the fact I wasn't decked out in finery, but there was no use. Not when the man standing in front of me reeked of days' old blood and sweat. All I could do was stare, dumbfounded. He wasn't at all what I expected. Somehow both worse and not as dangerous as I'd assumed.

He inclined his head at my words and agreed, "Your future mate."

The thought sent a shiver racing down my spine. The threat of being bound to a mate, this man in particular, had always been on the peripherals of my mind. I had been raised knowing it would take place eventually.

Eventually had come.

I'd had twenty years to ready myself, but if I had

51

twenty more, it wouldn't have prepared me for the savage man towering over me.

Decades of legend and lore from the whispers of servants and passing dignitaries hadn't done him justice. Even though I'd been groomed to be a queen my entire life, his aura of power radiated throughout the room. He didn't need the threat of the throne, or an elaborate crown, to assert his dominance the way I always had before I'd been cast out. And I wanted to slap the resulting impertinent smile off his face to mask my own insecurities. No one would have dared to take the throne from him, you could see it in his eyes; the way they gave warning without him having to say a word. That was why Father had gone to him for protection, even though it had been against both the Council and my mother's wishes. She'd wanted me to mate for love, according to what my brother told me.

It wasn't only his dominance that intimidated me. He was exactly the type of man old crones would warn their granddaughters about, in order to get them to behave. *Marry a good, kind man, they'd say. You don't want to be burdened with a brute.*

My mother had married such a man, and though I loved my father beyond reason, many people said it was why she died after giving birth to me. She was cursed after marrying a man with violence in his blood.

A man like Lord Blaque.

And I was following right in her footsteps.

Whether I wanted to or not.

"Princess," he said and knelt at my feet in such a way he made a mockery of the act. His lips remained in a firm line, everything about him hard and unforgiving. A man like him didn't need to kneel, but he did it anyway.

I didn't know what to say. I was so woefully unprepared. He took my hand in greeting, his lips grazing my skin. It had been so long since I'd been so close to anyone who wasn't bleeding that my heart stumbled in my chest.

"My lord," I said when I could speak again. It took extra effort to keep my voice even. "It's a pleasure to meet you. I apologize for the misunderstanding."

I couldn't show him any weakness. The stony look in his eyes and his massive build, not to mention the rumors about his first mate, told me he'd take any weakness and devour it like the finest meal, spitting my bones out the moment his appetite was sated.

He got to his feet slowly and I wondered if living in the North had frozen his expression, because I could glean nothing of what he may be thinking from his face. "Even if I'm a brute?"

Before I could respond and ask him what he meant, Gideon appeared in the doorway once more. He was out of breath and hurried to my side pressing a palm to my back. I couldn't tell if he was trying to reassure me or to keep me from running. "I see you've met," he said in a practiced tone. "I hope you've found everything to your… satisfaction."

Eyes still on me, Lord Blaque said, "Oh, I'm sure I will." He cocked his head as though considering. I stiffened, my skin beginning to crawl with an uncanny awareness that wasn't altogether unpleasant. I wanted nothing more than to put as much distance between us as possible. Then I realized, once we were bound to one another, there would be no such thing as distance.

My body a statue of granite, I didn't know whether to be insulted or relieved. A gauntlet had been thrown and he'd barely said a word. Though it was warm, and I was wearing more clothes than should be allowed, a shiver coursed through me at the challenge.

Or maybe, it was due to the hint of smile now present in those ice-blue eyes.

The shivers increased, and I tucked my arms protectively around my waist. Mostly to ward off the chill, but also to hide my hand, which was still tingling from his lips on my skin. "I'd best get ready for dinner," I said with false amicability. Ignoring his innuendo seemed prudent for the moment. Whatever political maneuvering my brother intended, The Dragon clearly wasn't so inclined. "The Queen is eager to introduce me to her mate." I decided to settle on relief and nod to both men as I made my escape.

Except, a hand on my arm halted my exit.

I turned to find Lord Blaque entirely too close.

"I'll escort you to dinner," he said.

There was no use in arguing, so I nodded and made a hasty retreat.

HOURS LATER, I turned to Leisha and tried to prevent my voice from wavering. "How do I look?"

Leisha, who sat on a chaise in front of the fire, patient as ever, tilted her face up from her sewing. The moment she saw me, her expression brightened. "Oh," she breathed, then went silent.

I grimaced. "That terrible?"

She set the sewing aside and came to me. "Oh, no, Elena." With her hands on my shoulders, she turned me to face the mirror I'd been avoiding. "Look."

I didn't want to. Part of me was afraid to look in the mirror and find the woman who failed to become queen. I'd been able to hide underneath plain clothes and drown myself with chores. At the temple I may have been suffocated, but I was safe. Nothing would happen to me there. I didn't have time for disappointment. From the moment I arrived, I'd been busy and hadn't stopped.

As I met my gaze in the mirror, time did just that,

then sped rapidly in reverse. In the span of a few seconds, I'd gone from the self-assured girl who'd learned the art of healing under the patient tutelage of the temple healer to the insecure princess who'd lost her way.

"What's the matter? You look beautiful."

"It's not that," I said, my voice barely a whisper, but I couldn't speak my fears. The last time I'd been in Aurelia, I'd run. I made a vow as I held my reflection: I was done running.

I'd face my fate, no matter what—or who—it was.

A knock came at the door and I ripped myself away with a frightened glance in its direction. As Leisha went to answer, I smoothed my hands down the thick material of my dress, even though there wasn't a wrinkle to be found. I shouldn't be nervous, but my hands trembled. Immortals mated all the time, for bloodlines, to increase power—both political and personal—and to ally powerful shifter clans. I was hardly the first woman to face an arranged binding.

Even knowing so, my heart tripped over itself as Lord Blaque stepped through the door, impossibly more handsome than hours before.

I hadn't had the time before to truly look at him, but as he spoke quietly with Leisha, I studied the man who was to be my future mate for the first time without panic clouding my thoughts. I could tell he reached over six feet at his full height. If we were standing face-to-face, he would no doubt tower over me. His tan leather coat was several shades lighter than his caramel skin and stretched over the broad expanse of his shoulders. A cape of the same hue billowed from his back. The sleeves of his coat were adorned with cuffs of curious thick scale-like armor. Soft breeches a shade lighter than his overcoat cupped powerful legs and disappeared into boots fashioned from the same material as his cuffs. It was a far cry from the ragged, bloodstained beast he'd been when we first met; I'd give him that.

His ice-blue eyes lifted to mine as I completed my examination and though I wanted, very much, to look away, I forced myself to keep his gaze. Thick, dark brown hair brushed his forehead. His face was as regal as my own. Feline eyes and a patrician nose were framed by the two slashes of his cheekbones and punctuated by the full line of his permanently smirking mouth.

He didn't seem like the monster rumor claimed him to be. If I knew nothing about him and had any inclination to be bound to another, he'd make a fine mate. My eyes caught on those lips. He may be a monster, but he was a beautiful one. If he hadn't been promised to me, he would have had no trouble finding another female to be his.

I had to stop thinking about his lips. I shook myself and remembered we weren't alone.

Two men stood at his back, though I knew from

many accounts he required no protection. He waved them away and Leisha scurried after, leaving us alone. I'd spoken with servants in Gideon's service about the goings-on in my absence and about Rhysander, but they could tell me little. The only thing I knew for sure was that as the last of his kind, he was the rarest of all shifters. As the oldest, his authority wasn't a question, but a certainty. It was why my father had chosen him, after all. They didn't have to tell me about his former mate. Everyone knew what happened to her.

Rhysander was a dangerous man, and he was tasked with being my protector. But who would protect me from him?

"Good evening, Elena," came his deep voice. He hadn't missed my blatant perusal because he gave me one of his own. I ached to cross my arms over my body to block his view, but I wouldn't give him the satisfaction. "I'll escort you to dinner."

His remarkable composure grated on my already frayed nerves, but I nodded despite my body screaming to run in the other direction. I made it across the room without stumbling and placed my hand in his, stifling a gasp at the unnatural heat emanating from his skin. It was as though he was lit from the inside out with an eternal flame.

He placed my hand on his forearm and guided me through the door. His two companions, who were waiting in the hall, followed close behind as we wound through the castle to the dining hall.

Lord Blaque didn't speak, and I refused to lure him into conversation, so the walk to the hall was silent and rife with all the unsaid words and thick with tension. Normally, I'd take my meals in my room to avoid the whispers and stares from the others. When he and I entered the crowded hall, all conversation ceased, and all eyes turn to us.

Uncaring or unaware of the attention, Lord Blaque led me to a high table where Seleste and Gideon were seated. The former shot me a covertly scathing look and the latter, a pleased one. I took my place next to my brother gratefully and planned to ignore my future husband on my other side.

But ignoring a man like him, I learned, was impossible.

Seleste surged to her feet. "Lords and Ladies," she announced in her simpering voice. "I'd like to make an announcement."

My stomach clenched on emptiness. I hadn't had a moment to prepare. I'd forgotten how the royals liked to put on a show, and Seleste most of all.

"As Queen." Was I imagining things, or did she put more emphasis than necessary on the word *queen*? "It is my great honor to announce that the arranged alliance between the Dragon-Clan and the Avians will take place tomorrow. To my everlasting pleasure, Lord Rhysander Blaque will be bound to Princess Elena Darkmoore."

She preened under the raucous reply from her captive audience; Seleste was always so much more gifted at commanding the attention of a group than me. Once the furor died down, she nodded and pressed a hand over her heart. "Not only will Princess Elena be joining the Dragon-Clan, but the Ursine alpha, Lord Darius, and I will also be bound. These alliances will further strengthen the shifters against the growing threats from the humans. In these dark times, know that we will stop at nothing to keep our people safe!"

My mouth had gone dry. I longed for a glass of wine, a sip of water, but the guards who tested my food for poisons had yet to appear. Lord Blaque was silent at my side and I was doing my best to ignore him. Did he dislike the humans as much as the rest of the Immortals in Acasia? Having spent so much time surrounded by them, healing them, I realized over the past three years that we weren't so different.

Most other Immortals didn't agree. The worst of us thought of them like pests that needed to be exterminated, or pets for entertainment. The vampires to the west saw them as cattle, something to feed on. It made me shiver to think about how they had great labyrinthine tunnels underneath the desert floors with human blood slaves shackled to feed on. I'd heard they used them for sport, setting them free to chase and capture.

Even the Fae, who kept to their easterly territory called the Vale, thought themselves above the humans. Like the vampires, they considered humans as playthings and loved to experiment on them with their ancient magick. I'd even heard of the Fae who thought it funny to trick humans into twisted contracts even more frightening than my own. My thoughts on humans, like my inability to shift, was something I didn't discuss with other Immortals.

Lord Blaque didn't seem like he'd disagree with the rest of the Immortals. He clapped along with the rest of those in the dining hall, his face as impassive as ever. What had he done that had let Seleste be rid of him without much of a fight? Knowing what I do of her, I would have thought she'd draw blood at the thought of losing something she considered hers. As Queen, it would have been a priority for her to marry the male from the next powerful line to beget more powerful queens.

Instead, she fawned over a man on her other side— Lord Darius—I presumed. He was a big, beefy man with palms the size of dinner plates and a brown beard threaded with red that was longer than my hair. Seleste twined her fingers in it and murmured to him in a low, seductive voice. It was no wonder she had so many suitors. Unlike me, she was glamorous, sensual, and vivacious. Again, my thoughts went back to the man at my side. Why had he so easily agreed to be bound to me instead, all those years ago?

"Something on your mind?" he asked, as though he could read my mind.

Before I answered, I took my time ordering my thoughts under the pretense of observing my surroundings as though checking for eavesdroppers. "Why did you agree to it?" I asked. "Being bound to me. You could have married the Queen. Become the King. You're wealthy, I know, but you could have had power. Connections. She's a powerful shifter and no one would have held you to the agreement you made with Father." The last may have betrayed more of my own insecurities than I would have liked.

"I've no need for more power, and no interest in being King. What I need is a wife who can produce an heir."

My tongue stuck to the roof of my mouth at his candor. "An h-heir?" I stammered. Whatever I had expected him to say, it wasn't that.

"You're of good breeding and despite your lack of a shifter form, you'd be a credit to the Dragon line." His gaze shifted from studying the court to me, and I wished I hadn't encouraged his conversation. "With the confirmed alliance between our two clans, it should stem the threat of uprising from the humans."

"So, you agree with my cousin, then? About humans being lesser than Immortals." I would worry about the heir comment later… much later.

"Those responsible for the baseless deaths of Immortals will be dealt with, but I don't hold an entire race responsible for the actions of a few." He positioned an arm behind me on my chair, effectively imprisoning me. Even though he wasn't touching me, I could feel the warmth emanating from his skin. "What about you, Elena? You could have stayed in the human temple, out of sight and out of mind and refused to be bound. You know the ceremony requires the agreement from both parties to prevent an unwilling union."

I met his gaze straight on. "My father is ill, my brother's position at court is tenuous at best, and my own life would be at stake unprotected. Either I accept you as a mate or fail my family again. There are no other options."

For some reason, instead of infuriating him, my answer pleased him. Though there was no hint of it on his lips, his eyes seemed to smile. "Then we have an understanding," he said with a nod as though my response answered all his questions.

I, however, was left with more questions than when I started. Servants appeared in the hall, their arms loaded with platters heavily laden with food. The scents of buttered vegetables and roast pig wafted throughout the hall. My mouth watered as the first course was served and wine poured. Even Lord Blaque's presence didn't dull my appetite.

The routine of food tasting was so ingrained I barely paid any mind to the men who were tasked with ensuring my food wasn't poisoned. I didn't know the identity of the castle guard who stepped forward to test my plate. He sipped my fresh glass of wine and tasted the course of roast pig and vegetables. When nothing happened, I took the glass of wine greedily, hoping to calm my nerves. As I brought it to my lips, I felt Lord Blaque tense beside me.

Before the wine could bathe my tongue, he ripped the goblet from my grasp, knocking the cup against my teeth and splitting my lip. Wine spilled, staining my dress and soaking my plate of food. I frowned at the ruined meal for a moment. Gasps went up from the tables closest to us and murmurs broke out.

Puzzled, I turned to Lord Blaque who'd gotten to his feet, his blue eyes brightening unnaturally as though he were filled with lightning. Recognition speared through me and before I knew it, I was on my feet and putting distance between us, reacting purely on instinct.

But he wasn't focused on me. His gaze was on the

guard who'd tasted my food. "Who sent you?" he demanded.

Confused, I glanced to the guard whose face had gone pure white. The first strains of unease trickled through me.

Lord Blaque vaulted over the high chair with staggering ease and slammed the guard to the ground with one hand on his throat. With his other, he reached for my goblet of wine and looked inside. A small swallow remained in the bottom. Beneath him, the guard gulped convulsively.

"Who sent you?" Lord Blaque repeated.

The guard could only shake his head. With his face set in an impassive mask, Lord Blaque brought my wine goblet to the guard's lips and forced him to swallow. Within seconds, blood poured from the guard's ears and nose. White froth bubbled from his lips.

Lord Blaque got to his feet and looked to me. "We complete the binding ceremony immediately," he said. "Before the person who tried to assassinate you succeeds, and I bury my mate instead of bedding her."

RHYSANDER

"Skip the ceremony, it's all a façade anyway. All you need is a couple incantations from a priest. Return to the North before it's too late," Alaric said.

It wasn't Alaric himself, but a magicked replica I'd summoned. It required powerful magick, even for me, to produce the spell, but it was a useful one. Called *mirroring* the spell allowed one to summon another to speak with, even over long distances, and show their visage on any reflective surface nearby. In this instance, Alaric's *mirror* appeared in a basin full of water at the side table in my quarters. Even as a replica, Alaric looked gravely worried after I relayed the story of what happened at dinner.

"I won't have one threat scare me away, Alaric. If I ran every time someone tried, I'd be running forever. I'll go through with the ceremony tomorrow, bed my mate, then I'll head for the Northlands and never return to this Goddess-forsaken place again."

Alaric frowned even more. "This isn't only your life anymore. You have a mate now you have to think about. Do you think she'll want you dashing off to battle at every spare moment?"

I prowled about my rooms wishing for my caves, for the mountain, my castle. The capital keep was too stuffy, full to the brim of useless things, and despite the wintery air outside, it was stifling hot. All I wanted was to leap from the balcony and soar the skies for a few hours, but I didn't dare leave the castle with my future mate sharing walls with the person who tried to kill her.

It was taking all of my restraint to keep from roosting on her balcony, and watching her as she slept, to make sure there wasn't another attempt made on her life during the night. The thought pleased my dragon. It wanted me to shift and take her in my arms while he kept her safe. Maybe the beast wasn't half wrong. If they were bold enough to assassinate her in front of the whole court, what would happen to her when she was alone without protection?

"Prince Gideon secured a guard watch for her rooms. No one but her maid will go in or out for the next twenty-four hours. Tomorrow afternoon we'll be bound in front of the entire capital, and then she'll be under my personal protection. I may not be an enthusiastic mate, but I won't let anything happen to her." Not when I needed her. My clan needed her.

Alaric's *mirror* looked like he wanted to argue, but he wisely bit his tongue. "And the guard gave no indication about who put him up to it?"

Smoke curled from my nose in a delicate filigree. "Not before he choked on his own poison. He refused to talk, but it could be one of my many enemies, or any of the enemies against the crown." Or both. There were many, Immortal and human alike.

The *mirror* image of Alaric opened his mouth to speak, but a flash from the corner of my eye distracted me. I rushed to the balcony doors and flung them open, thinking I'd catch a thief or an assassin scaling the walls of the castle, but no. Instead, I caught the flash of a cloak disappearing into the forest beyond the castle. Then, the sliver of a face—one I recognized. One who made my dragon quiver with excitement at the thrill of a chase.

"Excuse me, Alaric," I said over my shoulder, as I allowed my wings to form. I extinguished the magick that conjured the *mirror* and jumped from the balcony into the obsidian blanket of sky. My dragon hummed his approval, enjoying unleashing even a modicum of his power, relishing the endless dark that swallowed us up and carried us away from the cloistering oppression of the castle. It wasn't the Northlands, but it was an acceptable substitute for now.

I found her by the marshy bank of a creek, deep in the woods. Her skin blue from sitting in the freezing night air, but there was a smile on her lips and she reclined against a tree on the banks, her eyes closed and completely unaware of her surroundings. How easy it would be to kill her here. I could slit her throat with one claw and watch her blood stain the snow. Did she not realize how dangerous it was to be on her own?

I landed behind her, the sound muffled by the thick dusting of snow. As much as I wanted to wring her neck for risking her safety, I kept back and watched her, like I had in her father's room. It seemed I had a penchant for watching her, an urge I'd have to curb once we're bound and living together under one roof. It wouldn't do to be so consumed by her. I'd let it happen to me once, and I'd never fall victim to such idiocy again.

At first, I considered the possibility she was meeting a spurned lover for one last night of passion, but no one came. She merely sat and watched the water ripple over the rocks, seemingly enjoying the peace and quiet away from the castle. She wasn't the only one. Already the open spaces and the promise of the sky above were calming my nerves.

My dragon seemed content after the short flight, but I knew that wasn't the only reason. He felt her presence and reveled in the knowledge that she was nearby. If I had any control of the beast, I'd leash him up and give him a muzzle. Clearly he didn't have any common sense. This girl was trouble. The sooner she was bound and bred, the sooner she'd no longer be my problem.

She grew aware of my presence in increments. Because I was watching her so closely, I noticed when her shoulders inched up toward her ears and her muscles tightened. As she was readying herself to flee, I took a step forward, the frosted snow on the creek banks crunching under my boots. At the sound, she whirled around as though prepared to fight, her hand going to an impressive dagger sheathed at her side. Strange, considering most women abhorred violence.

"No need for that," I said smoothly, holding my hands up in supplication. "It's just me, Princess. Although I doubt that dagger would be much protection if your would-be assassin came back for a second try with friends in tow."

Before answering, Elena glanced back over my shoulder toward the castle. "What are you doing here?" she asked. Her hand was still resting on the dagger. It made me want to smile to think of her trying to use it on me. I wondered if she knew how to use the damn thing. She'd probably end up hurting us both.

"Wondering why you thought it a good idea to travel outside the protection of the castle walls on the same night someone tried to end your life." If my tone was harsh, so be it. Maybe she needed someone to frighten sense into her. We weren't bound yet, but as far as I was concerned, she'd become mine the day her family had promised her to me. And I didn't take well to someone trying to harm what was mine.

"There's still another sunrise before we're bound together, Lord Blaque, so I'd say the answer to your question is none of your business." Despite the chill, her cheeks blazed with fire. Her hand fisted over the butt of the dagger, but her gaze was steady, which surprised me. Princess Elena had some fight in her after all. In another lifetime, I would have enjoyed having a woman like her at my side. I *had* enjoyed having a woman like her at my side.

And look where it had gotten me.

"And I would say that making sure you stay alive until we're bound is precisely my business. Considering I've spent the last twenty years providing for the crown, it seems the least you could do to make sure to hold up your end of the bargain."

She colored even more, her jaw working in barely contained rage. I wondered if she'd been so passionate when she'd held court before her dismissal. The stuffy Council wouldn't have approved, I was sure.

"I appreciate the sentiment, but I can take care of myself," she answered, as she wrapped her cloak around her waist. "I want to be alone, if it's all the same to you. You'll have the rest of our lives to smother me, I'm sure."

I wanted to dip into her mind then, scent her thoughts, but I restrained myself. I knew all too well how easy it would be to drown in her. Opening a mental connection between us would make it easier to know what she was thinking, but harder to know where she ended and I began. Not all shifters could blend minds the way dragons could, and for good reason. It wasn't always safe. The mental connection was chaotic at best and psychotic at worst.

Forcing myself to turn my thoughts back to her, I said, "Unfortunately, that's a wish I can't grant, but I can wait with you until you're ready to return to the castle."

With a toss of her hair, Elena turned back to the water and plopped back down. I took that to mean she didn't object… or at least knew when she couldn't win. Good. That lesson would serve her well. I meant to get what I wanted. It would be easier on all of us if she wouldn't fight me.

Much as I didn't want to be intrigued by my soon-to-be-mate, I found myself amused by her irritation. I spent the next hour or so enjoying being away from the castle and listening to the sounds of the forest. My little mate spent it shivering and staring determinedly in the other direction. Her refusal to pay me any mind didn't bother me until I realized her mouth and the tips of her fingers had turned blue from the chill.

She glanced up, her face full of apprehension, when I stepped forward.

"No doubt you'd rather freeze to death than let me touch you," I said, "but allow me the small liberty of making sure you make it to the mating bed."

She scooted away from me. "What are you doing?" she asked. My dragon purred at her retreat. He liked it when she made him work for it.

I placed a hand on her ankle, and she gasped from the difference in temperature. "I'm going to make sure you don't turn into an ice block. Easy," I murmured. I felt my mind reaching for hers without bidding. Cursing myself, I tried to get it under control. The beast inside me wanted to know her, though. Wanted to feel her as I did, but I couldn't let that happen. When I had it under control, I gritted out, "I'm not going to hurt you."

She snorted, but let me wrap my arms around her waist, her body as stiff as stone. At first, she didn't seem to understand what I was doing, aside from the fact I was wrapping my own thin cloak around her. I could tell by the apprehensive look on her face that she didn't think the material was enough to do much good. Body heat would do little when the temperature was so low and her dress was damp from the snow on the ground.

"What are..." she asked again then surprise stole the

words right from her lips. Her eyes were level at my throat and she rubbed them when she caught sight of the scales there. No matter how many times she blinked, the scales didn't go away.

Like most shifters, I could phase into different degrees of my animal form. In this form, the scales provided a shield against weapons and the elements. I was also able to increase or decrease my body temperature to suit the environment. Which I did until Elena groaned and pressed closer to my warmth.

"You're doing an awful lot for a woman you've never even met before," she said when her teeth stopped chattering.

"You're the woman who may be the future mother of my child. I'm willing to do whatever it takes to keep you safe, Elena, which I can't do if you leave the protection of the castle. Promise me, no more forays into the forest unguarded. I don't want to stifle you, but I don't want anything to happen to your pretty little neck either." My gaze wandered down to the neck in question. I wondered what it would taste like, and my dragon wondered what it would be like to give her our mark.

Contrite, she turned her eyes back to the water. "Forgive me. I merely wanted some time away from all the people. I'm afraid I've gotten used to the solitude at the temple. Court life doesn't seem to suit me anymore."

"I understand. I feel the same way. The Northlands

can seem isolating, but if it's solitude you're looking for, then you'll enjoy my home."

"If I may ask, what *is* your home like? I'm afraid I've never been to the Northlands."

I closed my eyes as I gathered her close into my warmth. "My castle was carved into the mountain range that spans the city of Fellenor. Some say there are parts of it that go so deep into the rock one can get lost trying to find their way out."

"Is that true?" she asked.

"The crypts underneath the castle are immense and one could get lost if they don't know where they're going. But I've scoured every part of them. If you got lost, I'd find you." She shivered at my words.

"What about your people? I've heard you're the last full shifter of your clan. Is it true there hasn't been another full-blooded dragon born in decades?"

I knew the question was coming. She was too polite to ask me what had really happened to curse our people. But there was no way in Slaine I was going into *that* with her. "No there hasn't, but we're going to change that."

Her eyes met mine and held. The bond I'd been fighting roared up inside of me like a tidal wave. My dragon wanted her.

And I was afraid there would be nothing I could do to stop it.

7

ELENA

S tupid girl.

I should have left the moment he showed up. At least after we were bound together, we'd be in his castle with servants and other shifters around as a buffer. Out here, there was only us.

The forthcoming man before me didn't seem like the one who could murder his mate in cold blood. Were the rumors really true? I couldn't be sure. "I-I'd better get back to the castle," I said and was furious to find my voice trembled, not with fear, but with something much worse—curiosity.

There was a moment of tense silence, and then he nodded. "I'll escort you back." When I moved to put space between us, he said, "You have nothing to fear from me, Princess. At least not yet."

I didn't grace that comment with a response, but I also didn't argue with him when he took my arm in his. His warmth was too seductive to deny against the wintry chill pressing in on my cloak.

And he was right; someone wanted to kill me. He may be a beast, but he was a threat I could see. Whoever poisoned my wine could be someone close to me, someone I trusted, which scared me more than being filleted and roasted by the Dragon.

Mostly.

The castle was quiet when we approached, but the guard had more than doubled. Lord Blaque turned to nod at those who'd been waiting silently at the entrance to my quarters. After I'd nearly been poisoned, they'd taken shifts watching over my rooms, which was what made escaping so difficult…and welcome. I hated being under constant surveillance at the castle. At least when I'd been banished to the temple, I'd been left to my own devices.

The guards bowed to me, and I inclined my head to them in return. A maid appeared from the shadows, took a candle, and led them away. My ladies-in-waiting twit-tered excitedly as they appeared out of nowhere. I dismissed them with a wave of my hand and I was pleased to find that it didn't shake with nerves as my voice had.

The doors closed behind the last of the servants with

a sound of finality, with Lord Blaque and I alone inside. I should have said goodbye before he escorted me to my rooms, but I didn't want to make a scene in front of the servants. There was already too much gossip where he and I were concerned.

My dress swished at my legs, settling around me in a swirl of elegant fabric as I put distance between us. The preparation had seemed silly at the time, but in hindsight I was grateful I let Leisha make up my face and hair for dinner. With his imposing presence, I felt I had to have all of my best cards at hand to come out as the victor and the finery felt a bit like a mask.

"Why did you come back?" he asked, as he ambled about the room and studied my things. He paused, one claw rifling through my bag of paltry dresses I'd worn at the temple. "You could have stayed away and I wouldn't have forced the issue. You're a princess. I'm a beast. No one would have blamed you."

"My father had an agreement with you. Darkmoores don't go back on their word. And wanted to see him…at least one last time."

At the mention of my father, I turned from him and walked to the floor-to-ceiling windows that looked over the courtyard and our lands in the distance. I had never been beyond the palace walls, aside from my trip to the temple, but I loved my kingdom. From the mountains and the thick forests teeming with life to the oceans and plains on our borders. It was my home, my heart, and it was my duty to be their champion, their savior, no matter the cost. Even if the cost was everything that made me who I was.

His boots clicked against the marble floor as he crossed the room toward me. His presence wasn't seemingly malevolent, but there was an energy that surrounded him which put my nerves on edge, and had since the first time I saw him. It made me wish for a weapon. Like the dagger my father gave me when I first learned I would be Queen—or when I first understood the reality of what it meant. My tutor, Hilda, hid it from me, when I became more interested in swordplay than my lessons. She'd scolded my father behind his back for giving such a violent gift to a lady. As Lord Blaque drew near, bringing with him the scent of smoke, earth, and cinnamon, I was helpless to protect myself. Not that a dagger would prove much protection from a dragon.

"He spoke very highly of you," he said. "And please, call me Rhys." He growled the name, *Risseee*, like the thought of his name on my tongue would bring him pleasure. If that were the case, it'd be a cold day in Slaine before he heard it from me.

"Did you meet with him often?" The people below me went about their nightly chores, unaware of the sacrifices I would soon make to continue to keep them safe.

I'd failed them so many times; I didn't want to fail them again.

"Often enough." He propped an arm against the window next to me and I glanced up at him, taken aback by the soft expression on his face as he gazed at me. I blinked and then the expression vanished, causing me to wonder if it was a figment of my imagination. "He said you would have made a magnificent queen."

Underneath the heavy layers of my dress I was sweating, and my knees trembled, but my face was smooth as glass and my voice did not waver. He was much too close, but I would never let him know he affected me in such a way. "I suppose it's a good thing neither he nor my mother are here to see how far from Queen I've fallen."

"The Dragon-Clan has a saying: Don't let anyone steal your fire. There's a fire inside you, bright as the stars, beautiful as dawn. They can only douse it if you let them." His voice was melodic, soothing. Devious. The long days of travel and the fading adrenaline had my weary body swooning toward him. Certainly there wasn't any other explanation for my reaction.

The thick material of my dress was stifling, or maybe it was the heat that came at me in waves from his too-near body. I kept my gaze on my feet so that he did not see my wild eyes. It felt like the fire he spoke of would burn me from the inside out. Was it the heat coming from his body that made me feel like I was being slowly scalded? It couldn't be. He wasn't even touching me.

As soon as I thought the words, bare fingers caressed the curve of my jaw and my eyes closed, though, to my despair, not from revulsion. The pads of his fingers seemed to spark where they came in contact with the soft skin under my jaw. I couldn't contain the nervous swallow or the thready beat of my pulse. I remembered the decadent feeling of being in his arms and surrounded by that warmth all too clearly.

"We should…" I cut myself off, cleared my throat. "We should get some sleep. With the binding ceremony tomorrow, it'll be a long day for both of us."

His smile returned, dangerous and full of depravity I didn't quite understand. His claw reached out and sifted through my hair. "You know, I didn't want to be bound to anyone." That I hadn't expected. Before I could bite out a retort, he continued, "But I'm beginning to believe it may not be so awful after all."

My breath caught in my chest and his fingers glided down the smooth column of my throat in a possessive movement that caused my back to stiffen. His hand rose again and his thumb traced the full line of my lower lip. My mouth opened the smallest fraction, and I licked my lips without conscious thought, tasting him there.

"How kind of you to say," I managed wryly.

He watched the glide of my tongue along my lip, his

smile gone. "Oh, I'm not a kind man, Princess," he murmured. "Didn't you know?"

I didn't respond at first for fear of dislodging the thumb on my lip. One taste of him was more than enough to know that a second would be unwise. I've heard ladies speak of temptations such as these. Especially where Lord Rhysander was concerned. Rumor of his prowess was legend, according to the maid. I had no desire to cloud my mind even with such distractions.

"Lord Blaque," I said before my voice cut out.

When he didn't respond, I looked up and almost fumbled backward. His eyes were no longer a tranquil blue. They were bright and turbulent, like chaotic, angry waves after a violent storm. The hand on my jaw snaked to the back of my neck to jerk me forward against his hard body. My hands came up to catch my fall and land on the firm, tightly knitted muscles of his chest.

"Rhys—" I started to protest, but was unable to finish. Since when did I call him Rhys? The hard, insistent press of his lips against my own robbed me of all words and common sense.

I had been kissed before, not that Gideon or my tutors ever knew about those stolen moments, and I thought I knew everything there was to know about the act. Sloppy, wet things, kisses. I thought, at the time, I was preparing myself for this, when I would meet the man I was promised to and we would kiss for the first time. An immature part of me thought I could surprise him with my worldly knowledge based on my meager experience.

I was wrong.

Instead *he* surprised *me.*

Rhys guided me backward with one powerful movement, though I didn't notice it other than as a passing thought that it felt like walking on clouds. His hand caught against the wall and then his body was trapping me there. Could it be called a trap if you didn't want to leave it?

The moment his chest brushed against mine, and his tongue plundered my mouth, I forgot about keeping the upper hand and kissed him back.

My hands found their way into the incredibly soft material of his cape. It flowed around and over his powerful shoulders, shrouding us from the outside world. His smoke-cinnamon scent was all-encompassing, filling me up and making me drunk on it. That was the only excuse I had for drawing my hands down his chest, to his waistline, to tug the thick material of his shirt from his breeches.

Pure madness, I told myself as I slipped my hands underneath to the taut skin of his abdomen. The muscles there contracted against my tentative touch and he growled against my lips. *I liked that,* I thought as I swallowed the sound. I wanted more, more of his madness, his kiss. My fingers traced through the soft hair on his stomach and followed it up the hardness of his chest. My fingernails scraped over the flats of his nipples and he hissed, crowding me into the hard stone wall until my hands became trapped between us.

His own hands tugged at the strings binding my bodice together until they loosened and the material hung off my shoulders. His deft fingers divested me of the top entirely and cool air swirled around me. My nipples tightened in response and that sent a wave of awareness through me. I noticed the open door one of the maids had forgotten to bring to after they left. I heard the clang of servants in the hallway beyond and realized anyone could peer in at any moment.

Noticing my distraction, Rhys tugged the cloth of my chemise under my breasts and broke the kiss, leaving me feeling lightheaded and tender-lipped. He brought his head beside mine, nuzzling me cheek to cheek, his nose scenting at my hair. My hands were freed long enough to grip his long locks and then his lips were moving down my throat and chest, leaving a tingling streak of gooseflesh in their wake.

His hands cupped my breasts and my head knocked against the stone wall, one or the other sent sparks of light over my closed lids. Rhys crouched the slightest bit to bring his head level, then took one aching tip into his mouth and sucked deeply. I arched against him, unprepared for such a deliciously wicked onslaught. One hand held the other breast, loving it gently, fingering small, featherlight circles that rivaled the slick flicks of his tongue. His free hand skirted down the line of my leg, rough fingers dug in the flesh to bring the heavy skirts of my dress and underclothes up just enough that he could find the aching heat of my center.

The cavernous room swallowed my feeble moan as his fingers traced me through the thin material of my undergarments. He finished his attentions to the other nipple and kissed a path back up my neck, abandoning the wet tips of my breasts in the cool air, too sensitive and wanting.

He took my mouth again and this time I managed to prepare myself for the hard assault of his lips. I met him with a battle of my own, pressing against him, even as his fingers searched for the closures to my underthings. When that proved too difficult, he growled again, took the center piece in his hand and rent the material with a vicious tug.

My arms wrapped around his shoulders and I gave into the kiss until I didn't know where he ended and I began. He nudged my legs open with one powerful thigh and then his fingers delved into my wetness. I groaned into his open mouth and he broke apart to whisper, "That's it, pet," before he captivated me with another long, open-mouthed kiss.

One finger traced all the slippery, intimate parts of me under my dress and I was too consumed by desire to be wrought with inhibitions. A sting, then a feeling of fullness, an aching tenderness that shocked a gasp from my chest.

"Shhh," he said against my lips, "I've got you, Elena."

"Yes," I said before he resumed the kiss and the short, pulsing movements of his finger. I heard a clatter in the hall and my gaze darted to the door, but he didn't stop his ministrations. If anything, his fingers moved more insistently, fluttering against a part of me that shot fire over my entire body. Something inside of me sparked to life and muscles locked, starting with my toes, moving up to my calves, and then my thighs and stomach. My breath shortened, my chest ached, and he shoved my face in his neck so he could whisper in my ear.

"This body, it belongs to me. You see how it weeps for me? How it responds only to me?" He angled his finger in a come-hither gesture, tapping against the source of my desire, strumming me from the inside out and I stopped breathing entirely, my whole being focused on the movements of his hands. "This is the essence of our deal, Elena Darkmoore, future Queen of Acasia. You'll. Be. Mine. In every way and until the end of time."

I came apart against him, sobbing against his shoulder and his ruthless assault continued until he'd wrung every last drop of pleasure from me.

When naught but an echo was left, I looked up, my chest heaving and froze. Lord Blaque was standing in front of me, a respectable distance between us. His shirt was tucked into his waistband and his long, ebony hair was no more mussed than when he stood in front of my court. I glanced down at my dress to cover my disheveled state and found that nary a strap or ribbon was out of place. My garments were in pristine condition and I was not pinned against the wall like I was mere moments before. The only remnant from our interlude was the riot of sensation still tumbling through me.

Lord Blaque still had a hand cupping the side of my jaw, but his eyes were no longer stormy, but calm. Had I imagined it? Had it all be some sort of fantasy? A fantastical dream?

Underneath my gown, my body still quaked from the tryst. I could still feel him inside me, remember how he felt, hot and hard, against me. It couldn't have been my imagination.

The hand at my neck pulled me closer, and I stepped forward tentatively, afraid I might fall without the guiding presence of his palm. His scent wafted over me and my body again came to life. He rubbed his lips possessively over mine and I recalled his taste with startling clarity. I stifled the groan that rose in my chest and kept my hands between us to ward him off, even as I yearned for him.

"Damn it all to Slaine," he bit out.

His eyes were hard as stone when he pulled away and I realized I had completely underestimated him, despite the warnings. He smiled, though it was more like a slash of teeth, and it reminded me that he wasn't safe at all. There was a beast lurking just beneath the surface. "My dragon can't wait to be bound to you, it seems."

With that cryptic statement, he left me, body thrumming and mind whirling. His dragon?

What had just happened?

8

RHYSANDER

The following morning, I lingered longer than I should in my rooms. I was avoiding her. Which was what I should have been doing in the first place. I didn't need to get to know her to mate her, for fuck's sake.

My dragon couldn't be trusted to be in the same place alone with her. He had never reacted in such a way to a woman, not even to my former mate. With her, he had been quiet and still as the ice river. At times, I'd thought he'd gone dormant like the rest of my kind.

I shouldn't have let myself lose control, shouldn't have let my dragon forge the blending of minds. But he'd tasted her interest with her so close, scented her desire on the air, and his need had overwhelmed my control. So much so I couldn't resist blending my mind with hers.

The connection had been strong, stronger than I'd ever felt with anyone. I'd been a mere spectator as our minds wound together, and our impulses took over. I could still almost taste her; feel her skin under my touch. My fangs elongated, and my claws tore through my pants where my hands were gripping my thighs. Scales peppered my skin.

"Stars," I spat and finished dressing in ceremony finery, careful not to tear the fabric with my claws until they retracted. My father had worn the same when he was bound to my mother. I'd forgone the tradition with my first ceremony, but I donned the gleaming white cloak and breeches this time to honor Elena's station as princess.

The sooner we got this over with the better. The capital was driving me mad, that was all. Once we were back in the cool, clear air in the Northlands where things made sense, my dragon would be back under control.

The ceremony was to be held mid-afternoon. Before then, I needed to speak with my future mate. What happened last night couldn't happen again.

For both our sakes.

HER ROOMS THRUMMED with activity when I could slip away from my own preparations a few hours later. Maids and guards milled about, their chattering a low buzz in the air. They quieted as I grew closer.

"Leave us," I ordered.

Once the room emptied, I lingered a moment, mired in the scent of her. Much like I had been to her voice, I was drawn to her scent. I wanted to bury my nose in it and paint it on my scales. If I had less of a hold on my control, I would have found her, put her thighs over my shoulders and tasted her scent from the source.

Furious with myself, and with her for evoking such urges, I turned and strode to the bathing rooms. Steam billowed from the semi-opened door, carrying her scent mixed with floral notes to my twitching nose. I followed it without a thought, cursing myself the entire way.

I find her in a cavernous soaking tub more the size of a small pond. She'd arranged herself along the far side, her head resting against the wall and her body floating in steam and bubbles. She couldn't have looked more appetizing if she tried. I wondered if she'd let me take a bite, then gave myself a brief shake. It was getting to where I didn't know if my thoughts were mine... or the dragon's.

Our shifter form represented the deepest, animalistic versions of ourselves. Paired with magick older than living memory, they were powerful. For weaker shifters, they were sometimes overpowered by their animal selves, ruled completely by their inner beasts. It seemed when it came to Elena, my beast wanted to come out and play.

Something in the air must have alerted her to my presence, because she shifted, making the water ripple out away from her, and opened her eyes. They widened even farther when she saw me take a seat at the edge of the bathing pool.

"You shouldn't be in here," she said, panting a little. I tilted my head, watching her breasts flirt with the top of the water. I inched closer, hoping to see her nipples revealed through the bubbles. As though she knew what I was thinking, she slipped farther into the frothing water, obliterating my view.

"Shouldn't I?" I responded, when I could pull my gaze back up to hers, which was flashing with fire.

"If you don't mind, Lord Blaque, I'd like to get ready for the ceremony." When I didn't immediately agree to her request, she added, "Without your help," through gritted teeth.

"Much as I'd enjoy assisting you, that's not why I'm here."

She gestures with an impatient hand. "By all means me why you're here, take your time."

I wondered if she knew her brown eyes turned to slits when I annoyed her. "I wanted to talk to you about what happened last—"

"We need not talk about it," she said before I could

finish. Was she embarrassed? I almost purred. There were delicious acts my dragon wanted from her that would make her more embarrassed than one kiss.

The candles she had lit on the lip of the bathing pool flickered across her face. I enjoyed seeing her bathed in flame this way.

"We do. I must apologize. I was not... as in control as I would have hoped."

Her lips parted for a moment before she pressed them together. "You weren't in control?" she asked.

I scrubbed a hand over my hair. "My dragon finds you very appealing. Sometimes if our dragon finds a potential mate... tempting, it will forge a mental bond. We call it the blending of minds. That's what happened last night." She straightened at my words, her expression turning pensive. "Needless to say, it wasn't how I intended to begin our... relationship, nor do I want to complicate it further."

"Our relationship," she responded, echoing my tone, "would be well served if your dragon could control itself in the future. I don't enjoy having my mind invaded like that. Can you, I don't know, stop him?"

"I'll do my best," I said.

"Is that all you wished to talk about?"

"One would think you're trying to get rid of me, Princess."

She gave me a tight smile. "That would be difficult considering we're about to be bound together for life."

THE ENTIRE KINGDOM traveled overnight to witness the binding ceremonies. Word traveled fast amongst shifters, and a royal wedding was the most exciting thing to happen in decades. Scores of them were visible through the windows to the balcony where it would take place as I waited in the attached room, my expression reserved. Thoughts of the previous night kept replaying repeatedly, despite my best efforts. Seleste and Darius' binding ceremony happened first, which made the day drag.

I sensed the moment she walked through the door with her ladies in attendance. I couldn't help but look, it was as though my dragon had become sentient and taken control of my body. My head turned, and our eyes met. I felt the connection, the blending of minds, like a wave of warm spring air over my exposed skin. It would be easy to dislike her if she were more like my first mate. Maybe once I got to know her more, I'd find they had more in common and this... obsession of sorts would resolve itself.

Elena's eyes widened at my attention and I sensed her body stiffen underneath the flowing white material of her dress. She'd worn my colors instead of the traditional Darkmoore red. I appreciated seeing her in Dragon-Clan colors more than I should. She tensed long enough to be sure I wouldn't try to ensnare her in more visions, then ignored me, which only intrigued me more.

She didn't want to be my mate, but she wouldn't run from her fate either. I'd told Alaric I didn't want a bride with a backbone—but maybe I'd been wrong.

Once the preparations were complete, I'd had enough of her pretending I didn't exist. We'd have plenty of that after the ceremony.

"Ready?" I asked from behind her. She started, but only for a moment and then turned to face me.

Being this close to her reminded me of how she'd felt in the vision. If possible, she was even more radiant knowing she was about to be mine. Her brown eyes were expertly lined with kohl, making them seem dark and secretive. Something shimmered on her cheeks and painted her full lips. My hands twitched at my sides, and I stopped myself for reaching for her to draw her close.

She nodded and surprised me by holding out her hand. I took it, ignoring the spark of energy that coursed through me as I placed it on my forearm. The blending of minds made one more sensitive to a potential mate. Something I didn't need considering how intriguing I already found her. At a signal from Gideon, two attendants pushed opened the double doors leading out to the balcony. A cheer rose from the crowd.

The priest addressed the crowd first, speaking about the grand sacrifices of House Darkmoore and the beauty and bounty of Acasia. Then, he thanked the mighty Dragon-Clan for their protection and loyalty. The crowd cheered once more and bouquets of flowers soar through the sky.

The priest paused his spiel to welcome us forward. She pressed against me as we moved out onto the balcony to jubilant screams from the crowd. She waved with her free hand, a serene smile plastered on her face, then turned to face me as the priest came to stand before us. Her brother, Gideon, wore no expression in the background. I was grateful we'd be going back to the Northlands. I got the impression her brother may be supportive of the match, but he wasn't a fan of me.

The priest spoke in an ancient language that only the clergy understood, as they passed it down from generation to generation since the Goddess created Acasia. Elena frowned ever so slightly, and I realized she must not know the words.

"I pledge myself to you, heart of my heart and soul of my soul," I said through our connection in her mind. She glanced in my direction, her frown deepening. "I vow in front of all who will stand witness, that I am yours until the last light of the last day. I bind myself to you, heart of my heart and soul of my soul. I will fight for you, I will die for you, and I will love you until the last light of the last day."

I'd vowed these words once before, when I'd been much younger and more receptive to adhering to them. Once I realized they were empty promises, I no longer gave them any weight. It didn't seem to be the same for Elena, who must no doubt be thinking of her parents, who'd married for love, much to the chagrin of the Council. Royals rarely married for reasons other than for the crown. She'd do well to learn that sooner rather than later.

Her voice rang out clear and strong over the clamor, "I pledge myself to you, heart of my heart and soul of my soul. I vow in front of all who will stand witness that I am yours until the last light of the last day. I bind myself to you, heart of my heart and soul of my soul. I will fight for you, I will die for you, and I will love you until the last light of the last day."

Despite my feelings about taking another mate, I liked the sound of her promises. My dragon liked them even more. A growl, borne from the most primal depths inside of me, erupted from my chest and reverberated through the space between us. I used my grasp on her hand to yank her against my chest. She frowned up at me and opened her mouth to admonish me, no doubt, when I cut her off mid-thought with my lips.

She made a sound of protest, but didn't move to back away.

Her hands came to my shoulders, and the whole celebration silenced. The only thing I heard was the sound of our vows echoing around us. Her voice and mine, combined, the tones blending together to become one. I felt her knees give. My arms tightened around her and lifted her off the ground and pressed her to me.

It wasn't a few moments later that she realized I never set her back down.

She broke away from me to look down and saw that we are soaring above the audience, my large ice-blue wings keeping us aloft. Her hands tightened on my still-human shoulders and I chuckled.

"Don't be afraid, Princess. It would not serve me well to let you come to harm and break my vows so soon."

"If you don't put us down, I'm afraid I may have to," she told me, though her voice was barely above a whisper.

"Trust me," I said.

She closed her eyes again, and I remembered even though she was a member of the Avian-Clan, she'd never taken wing. The wind rushed by and she huddled closer to my warmth. What a sight we must be, a half-dragon and princess flying above the kingdom. If the citizens wanted a spectacle, we were giving them more than they expected.

"Where are you taking us?" she asked.

"I did not want to tarry with the well-wishers and sit through the twelve-course meal," I answered, once again speaking directly in her head. She didn't argue with my invasion of her mind this time. "There would be too many opportunities for enemies to poison you once more. I intend to have you in my bed and under me before they can."

9

ELENA

The silk of my dress did little to protect me against the frigid breeze and despite that, my core heated and a full body flush spread over me. His flight slowed and the dip in height caused my belly to leap. My fingers dug into his shoulders and I pulled closer. Then his feet were on the ground and he lowered me down his front until I could touch. I didn't immediately let go, my fingers gripping his cloak.

"Come, Princess," he said as he drew away slightly.

We were on a smaller balcony on the other side of my castle. He sensed the moment of hesitation and tugged on my fingers. I followed, stepping through the open double doors into his private rooms.

We designated the largest and most ornate of the guest rooms for his use during his stay. It consisted of three large quarters. One living area with a statuesque fireplace, sumptuous couches and stocked liquor cabinet. Next to it was the bedroom. I peered into the open doors into the dark blue interior. I imagined him in his mussed bedclothes, spread out against the blue silk, bare-chested and resplendent in sleep.

I tried to steer the conversation away from the bedroom. Not that I was trying to avoid it; I knew consummating our bond was inevitable, but I wasn't eager. Not when that eagerness was also tainted with a hint of fear. "You think whoever poisoned my food is still after me?

He unbuttoned his shirt, starting at the top. The sudden protrusion of his magnificent wings had split through the material. Shreds of it flickered around him as the wings retracted. His bared muscles bunched and contracted under the fabric. "I think if they're determined to kill you, they won't stop after one attempt. They'll try again until they succeed."

"But there's no reason to kill me. I'm no threat to the throne. Now that we're bound, I'll be leaving for the Northlands. It makes no sense." I should have stayed in the temples where I had been all but forgotten. If it weren't for my father, I would have. Rhys would have married Seleste and I could have lived out my days in oblivion.

Rhys tossed the tattered shirt on the nearest couch

and prowled toward me, clad only in his dark breeches and the dragonhide boots my maids were swooning over. His chest was as I remembered from the illusion. Broad and tan and magicked with an iridescent sheen of scale. The fire flickered over its surface, drawing my reluctant eyes. My fingers itched to trace them to see if they felt like scales or skin.

"I never wanted Seleste." He stood in front of me then, eyes even more blue and locked with mine. When I tried to move away, his clawed hand gripped my chin. His consciousness slithered across mine, leaving me bared and exposed.

I jerked away and said through gritted teeth, "Don't do that. I don't like having you in my mind that way."

"We talked about your father," he said, ignoring my protests and reading my mind again. "He's as good as gone, Elena. You should mourn him now and be done with it."

My fists clenched at my sides. "If you think this is how you'll convince me to go to bed with you, you're sorely mistaken."

He smirked, but took a step back. "I won't have to convince you, pet. If it bothers you so much, once you conceive an heir you can send for your father to come stay with us in the Northlands."

Mouth dry, I swallowed hard, trying to form words. I'd done my best to bury the comment he'd made at dinner about children until now. "That… feels like bribery. Is that how you deal with all your mates?"

He lifted a shoulder, not taking the bait. "What are relationships if not a barter? I've found it's better to be direct. You have needs, so do I. At least this way there won't be any claims of miscommunication."

I wanted to cure my father more than anything. I couldn't do that if he was here in the capital, wasting away in that stuffy room like he'd been forgotten. If I could have him with me in the Northlands, then I could work on healing him with my own hands. Or at least be with him when he died.

"I take it we have a bargain?" he asked, no doubt having read my mind again.

"Stop doing that!"

"Do we have a bargain?" he repeated.

"What is it with you and making bargains? Have you been socializing with the faeries? Yes, fine. If you'll help me cure my father."

"Deal," he bit out, then shackled my wrists with his hands. "Enough talking."

His eyes shuttered closed and his chest rumbled against my own where we were pressed together. My nipples constricted, and my fingers constricted on his biceps. The state of arousal he left me in after his intrusion into my bathing room roared back triple fold.

Words and common sense were feeble against this adversary.

He laid his cheek against mine, rubbing it up and down and he *purred*, "Oh, pet, I feel how you ache for me."

"I do no such thing," I denied, even though I was strung so tight one movement would shatter me.

Warmth slicked along my neck and ended at my ear. I bit my lip to contain the groan even as his teeth nipped and he soothed the sting with his tongue. "You need not lie to me, Elena. Your body speaks the truth even if you do not." He backed away, taking one of my hands in his. "Come."

And I feared I might do just that before we even made it to the bedroom.

At a loss for words, I followed him through the doors and into the dark recesses of his bedroom. His essence of cinnamon and smoke was doubly strong. I inhaled deeply, needing to make it a part of me.

With a wave of his long, tapered fingers, Rhys lit the small fire in the hearth with no match or kindling. My eyes met his in surprise. "I must admit you're nothing like I expected."

He toed off his boot and strolled back to my place beside his bed. "And what were you expecting?"

"I'm not sure."

He looked down and took my hands in his, my own

milky skin against his caramel brown. "There's not much to know." He pressed a kiss to my palm that I felt in other, more sensitive areas.

Thinking of the rumors, I said, somewhat breathily, "Somehow I don't believe that."

With a sigh, he said, "What would you like to know, pet?"

Put on the spot, I struggled to think of a pertinent question. Truth be told, I was stalling a little. What little intimacies I'd had in my life had not prepared me for what was to come.

Noticing my discomfort, he said, "Perhaps we should stick to not talking. We seem to get along well in that respect."

Rhys got to his bare feet to corral me toward the bed. He urged me toward the bed and I refused to take to it like the weak virgin I was. Instead, I turned to offer him my back. "The laces. Would you mind? I can't reach them."

He murmured his approval. "I enjoy this color on you." His fingers slid up the exposed skin of my back, so slowly that I felt each finger as it passed over every ridge of my spine.

"It is the color of your house, isn't it?"

"Yes." He reached for the ties and pulled. The material at the front of my dress loosened and caught on my breasts. My fingers quaked, but I let the dress fall, pooling at my hips.

I turned to face him, but he stopped me with an arm around my belly, pulling my back flush against his bare chest. I shivered against his heat.

"Lord Blaque?" I asked. I'd worked up the courage for this moment throughout my preparations for the binding ceremony. If I put it off, I may very well lose my nerve. Which was the one thing I couldn't allow in his presence.

"There's no rush. I mean to bed you as many times as it takes."

If I were being honest, I wasn't altogether put off by the prospect. If the vision his dragon had shared with me was any sign, I wouldn't lack for pleasure from the experience.

I stilled under his roaming hands, allowing them to map the expanse of my back with the soft, heated touch of his fingertips. He gathered the length of my hair and arranged it over one shoulder so he could kiss the curve of my neck. I arched to the side, allowing him access, and one of his hands stole in front of me to cup the tender weight of one breast in his big palm.

He licked a path up my neck and heat washed over me that had nothing to do with the crackling fire in the hearth. Going to bed with him would have been so much easier if I didn't enjoy his touch so much.

"Give in to me. Let me take care of you," he whispered in my ear.

The want for him suffused my being, and I let it take over all rational thought like I had in the illusion he wove. Focusing on the rough touch of his work-hewn palms over the silk of my skin, or the wet bite of his kiss, was easier than worrying what might come of my submission when the sun rose. It was better than worrying about what parts of me he might unearth and plunder to make his own.

I turned to face him, my lips rising in askance, and the warm thrust of his tongue gave me all the answers I needed to know. He nipped at my lip, took it between his teeth, and then soothed away the sting. The tips of my breasts pressed against the warm skin of his chest and my toes curled in the elaborate sandals I'd worn for the binding ceremony.

My fingers fluttered over his chest in an immature show of nerves. Many monarchs before me were bound to those they did not choose. Allegiances were formed. Whole populations were saved. It was my duty as a royal to ally myself with a mate who could be of the most use. I was grateful we didn't stick to the traditions of old where the consummation had to be witnessed by other royals.

I never thought I'd want him as much as I did.

I never thought he would make my blood burn or my heart race.

He swiped a hand behind my knees and I threw my arms around his neck for stability. He lifted me as though I weighed no more than a feather and carried me to his unkempt bed. As he laid me down on its softness, I changed my mind. I was glad the servants hadn't switched out his bedclothes because his scent surrounded me in every direction. It emanated from the sheets at my back and his hard body to my front until I was dizzy with it, consumed by it.

Rhys followed me down, covering my small body with his own. My legs tangled in the remaining material of my dress and he removed it with aching slowness, his eyes on mine as his fingers trailed down my stomach and over my hip, then down the length of my legs, leaving me completely bare to his gaze. I allowed him to look his fill, and my body did not tremble. He fit himself between my legs, the movement both aggressive and exhilarating.

He propped himself on his arms above me. "Don't be afraid. I won't hurt you."

I squared my shoulders as much as I could and met his stare. "I am not afraid."

"Such a spirited little princess you are." He surprised me with a slow, languid kiss. "I didn't think I'd like it."

"I do endeavor to please you, my lord," I said dryly.

I thought he might say something witty, but he was too busy nibbling at my lips. His breeches were soft against my thighs. I experimented with the sensation and wrapped them around his waist, pulling him against me with the strength of my legs.

"Yes." His low moan did wicked things to the pulsing deep inside of me. It was all he said, but the word was full of unsaid things. The deep, low moan emanated from his chest, full of want and need and desire... for me.

The tips of his fingers mapped the hills and valleys of my ribs, growing ever closer to the straining buds of my nipples. My back arched to bring him closer, but his fingers stilled just underneath where I wanted them most. I brought my hands to his biceps because I needed something, anything, to hold onto to weather the onslaught.

His mouth stole down my throat and over my collarbone. My breath stuttered to a halt, and his lips pulled into a grin against my skin. "Where would you like me to touch you first?"

Was everywhere a possibility? I wondered, before I recalled that he could hear my every thought.

"Your wish," he murmured.

I expected it would be more of the same from the vision; in fact, I was quite looking forward to it, if I was being honest. But instead of going where I wanted him, where I needed him, he moved down my stomach.

"What are you doing?" I breathed.

He pressed a kiss to my hip, and my hands went automatically to his long, thick hair. "I'm giving you what you need."

I didn't contradict him. I couldn't even if I wanted to. Not with the waves of need coursing through me with increasing urgency. His hands moved to my hips and started the slow journey down. He positioned my legs so he could settle his wide shoulders to fit between them. He was so close to me that I could feel his breath fanning against the wetness there. Anticipation built until I was fairly trembling with it.

Then, he pressed a long, wet stroke of his tongue against the center of me and I gasped, my legs widening of their own volition. There was a delicious wickedness in the wide spread of my legs. Like before when he had me pressed against the wall where anyone could see. He must delight in having me vulnerable, at his mercy.

"You know I do," he said in my mind.

One strong arm pinned my bucking hips, and I lost my protests in the flick of his tongue and sting of his teeth. The restraint incited the growing need in my stomach and my breath caught on a strangled scream of frustration. Confusion and excitement warred inside me as I fought against the rising storm of sensation.

"That's it, pet," he said. "Let it come."

One hand shifted, going between my legs to join his devious tongue. He traced my entrance and my hands flew up to grasp the bedposts for stability, certain whatever he had planned next would shatter me.

He teased me, flirting with quick flicks and gentle caresses until I could cry from annoyance. "Please," I begged on a moan. "Rhys, please."

Then one stroke, almost too deep and hard for comfort sent me over the edge. I felt it doubly. Once from my view, the physical pleasure I experienced from release, and yet another from his, but only for a split second. The enjoyment he got from watching me, doing it to me. The pleasure-pain of his own throbbing desire. All of it had me seeing stars.

The pleasure didn't abate from the climax. Instead it grew. I wanted him, if only to appease it. When I regained control of my limbs, I cupped his face with my hands and pulled gently, bringing his hot, hard body over mine.

He took my mouth with wild abandon, slanting his head over me, his tongue plundering and ruthless. Much like the man himself.

The deep, mind-numbing kiss caused the world around us to spin off into oblivion. I didn't want it to end. Then, a brief moment of pressure and the sense of intrusion spiraled me back to rationality. There wouldn't be any going back if we continued. The words balanced on the tip of my tongue. It would have been easy to go back on the agreement—well easy for me.

But, I didn't, I couldn't. Too much relied on me. And if I admitted it to myself, a part of me craved him. I bared my throat to receive his mark. He sealed his lips against my pulse point and his tongue flicked out, before his teeth pierced the skin. I winced, expecting pain beyond measure, but I was shocked by the flood of pure pleasure, even more exquisite than what I had already experienced.

My eyes popped open, my nails dug into the prominent muscles of his back, and then there was a burn between my legs, one that stole the breath from my chest.

"Stars," he muttered against my throat as we became one. "Elena."

I didn't respond, I couldn't. Then he pushed fully inside, assuaging the sting of pain by murmuring endearments in my ear. He whispered in the ancient language, enchantments, curses, I didn't know. And after a few moments... I didn't care. He was big and hard and completely inside of me.

All around me.

Overwhelming in his intensity.

As he pumped inside of me until I surprised us both with another climax, I had enough presence of mind to realize there would be no going back.

We were bound together.

10

RHYSANDER

I dressed and left the princess sleeping in my bed before the sun rose. The castle was quiet as a tomb. Most of the servants shied away as I ambled to the upper levels. I could have taken to wing from the same balcony where we'd landed the night before, but I wanted to put as much space between Elena and I as possible. The blending between our minds was a constant throb now that we were bound, but it dulled a little with the distance.

I stopped a servant, whose eyes bulged at my hand on their arm. "Please inform Prince Gideon the Princess and I will leave at first light. Have our coaches prepared and my men informed."

"Yes, Lord Blaque," he replied with a stammer. "Of-of course."

I'd *mirror* Alaric before we left to keep him abreast of our travels. With the attack in Braedon, I didn't want to linger away from home too long. Now that my contract with King Baron was satisfied, the men I'd appointed to the southern borders of the realm would also return with us. A point of contention I'd not allowed the crown to sway.

Shrugging the thoughts away, I launched myself from a barren room I'd broken into at the highest levels of the castle. The smattering of capital serfs were but smudges beneath me as I urged my ice-blue wings to strain higher and higher. Soon I'd have more of my people in the skies alongside me. There'd be so many Dragon-Clan, we'd blot out the stars.

Those among my advisors thought my plan foolish. The curse on me couldn't be broken.

But I didn't plan to outwit the curse.

I planned to break it.

And my pretty mate was the key.

As the sun rose on the edge of the horizon, I tipped my wings to carry me to the balcony's edge. Elena was awake, I could see through the hazy glass windows. She was still in bed, wrapped tight in my sheets, but other-wise naked. Her bare shoulders were visible above where she fisted the material in her hands, as well as the swells of her firm breasts.

I could have her now, if I wanted.

I'd been inside her mind and I knew she'd bend to my will with the slightest enticement. She'd been as hot as dragon flame beneath me, around my cock. Remembering it had my fangs lengthening and my dragon purred.

He'd like it, too. So much, he'd claimed her as his own.

It hadn't been a part of my plan to brand her with my mark. The magick between mates is ancient and as complicated as court etiquette. In short, branding your mate comes from the shifter's animal. It's a sign the beast preferred the match and wanted to make it known to the world. If I had a choice in the matter, I wouldn't have marked her as mine. Most people saw the sign of a brand as the sign of true mates, which was ludicrous. True mates were the thing of faerie tales. Worth less than a promise from the Prince of Fae himself.

It didn't matter. Beasts were fickle creatures, prone to fits of temper and whim. He merely felt the power from her family line, as I did, and knew the alliance was a beneficial one. He marked her to protect that alliance. Maybe he was cleverer than I gave him credit for.

Perhaps the mark would make her even more amenable to the arrangement. The sooner I had her belly swollen with a child, the better. I planned to devote myself to the effort until we had several hatchlings to carry on the Blaque name.

Feeling markedly more relaxed after the flight I strolled into the room. Elena jerked the sheets up to her neck. "Lord Blaque!" she exclaimed with a squeak. "The servants said you were preparing to leave."

"I wish I wasn't naked," her thoughts called out to me.

"I'm glad you are," I answered.

Her eyes widened, and I chucked. "As soon as you bid your father farewell, we leave for the Northlands." Dropping my voice an octave, I added, "We'll save the nakedness for when we get to Fellenor."

She ignored the last comment and said instead, "Thank you. I-I'm grateful. He means a lot to me." I didn't have to read her mind to know that was true.

Elena's cheeks were flushed pink as she got to her feet, the swaths of sheets rippling around her body. With aching tenderness I wasn't sure I deserved, she moved to my side and kissed my cheek. The affection resonated deep inside me, rippling like stone disturbing water. I didn't want to be disturbed. I liked my waters clear and calm.

"I need to see to my men," I said gruffly, cutting off the moment. "I'll wait for you in the stables."

Her lips parted in question, then she pressed them together with a nod. "Very well. I'll be quick."

"Take your time." I caught sight of my mark on her neck as she turned away and my chest was alight with internal flame. I choked down its embers and ignored the roaring of my dragon, who urged me to pin her to the bed with my teeth and make her ours again.

She dressed quickly and quietly. The door closed behind her when she was done, and I breathed a sigh of relief. The tether I had on my beast was tenuous at best. I wanted her bred, but on my terms, when I was in control. I'd never let myself lose control again. Not when it cost me everything I held dear.

"You went through with it, then?" Alaric drawled, his countenance rippling on the surface of water I had pooled in the sink.

"I don't know why you sound so surprised."

"After Valeria, I never thought you'd find another mate."

Her name echoed throughout the room, and I froze in the midst of packing my things. In the years since she died, the members of my court had spoken of her so little, hearing her name spoken aloud was a shock. "Neither did I," I murmured.

"I hope it works out for you. I mean that. I'm eager to meet her."

I cleared my mind of my first mate. Memories of her were a black road I'd be best served by not revisiting. "Provided that we don't run into another band of rogue humans, we should be there by week's end."

"We've had no reports of attacks in the Northlands, but they've never ventured so far away from their territory. Do you truly believe they'll risk crossing the ocean to retaliate?"

"I don't know what to believe anymore. Tensions have been rising against our people since long before we agreed to protect Aurelia's southern borders from their vengeance. It may be that the time has come for them to place all the blame on us."

"Regretting the promise to Baron yet?" Alaric asked. There was a teasing note to his voice, but the meaning behind the question wasn't without reason. There were plenty of female shifters I could have mated with, who wouldn't have brought the wrath of the humans down on our clan.

But none from as powerful a line as Elena. None with as close a tie to the throne, and therefore our ancestors, as her. None who ever caused me to doubt my vow to live the rest of my days alone, locked up in my castle, dooming my people to extinction.

"We didn't have another choice."

"You always have a choice."

"No, you always have a choice. You left your kingdom without a second thought. If I leave, my people are the ones with no choice."

"I won't take that personally. Anyone would be rather put out after shackling themselves to another for the rest of their days." I couldn't tell from the mirror alone if the jab had offended him. I regretted it nearly the second it spilled from my lips. Alaric's history was as complicated as my own, and I had no right to judge.

There wasn't an Immortal on the planet who didn't have a tragic story to tell about their past, and his was more tragic than most.

"I apologize. That was wrong of me to say."

He changed the subject, and I knew all was forgiven. "We've doubled the guard around the castle and in the crypts since the attack in Braedon. If they dare attack, they won't make it out unscathed. I have to tell you, I'll be more at ease when everyone is back safe."

"That makes two of us. Any other happenings I should be aware of?"

"We've had reports of a vampire and a solitary fae in the area," he answered.

"Really? That's unusual."

"Everything these days is unusual. None of the

Immortal races are stable anymore. Something is brewing."

I wasn't ignorant to the tensions between the Immortals and the humans, or even between the Immortals themselves. The curse had so long been my focus; I'd had no time to worry about the rest of the world going to Slaine. Once we broke the curse, I'd figure out how to save us from everyone else. There wouldn't be a Dragon-Clan to fret over if we didn't.

"We'll deal with it when it comes. But if any of them show threatening behavior, you have my permission to deal with them as you see fit." It wasn't often vampires or fae ventured so far North.

"If you don't mind, I'll have Raiden handle the fae, should they make an appearance." His expression in the *mirror* was grave, but I didn't pry.

"Of course." There was a knock at the door and a servant stuck his head through the door at my call.

"The carriages are ready, my lord," he said with a bow.

"Thank you." At my motion, they closed the door behind them. "I must go, friend. *Mirror* if you run into any trouble."

"Safe travels," Alaric said.

I could only offer his reflection a grim nod. He was right, something *was* brewing, something even worse than the curse that tormented my people. With so few

Dragon shifters left, if a war were to break out among the Immortals and humans, those who depended on me would be more vulnerable than ever.

It had never been so vital to produce an heir and break the curse.

11

ELENA

I'd never been so forlorn for my lack of a shifter form. I was deathly sick of the swaying carriage and makeshift bed, cranky from lack of sleep, and growing frozen by the rapidly chilling air the father north we went. Rhys was unfazed, both by the frigid weather and bruising pace his men set, though I didn't see much of him on the first day's ride.

I didn't realize when we left the capital how many men he'd traveled with, but I learned nearly an entire company of them followed him everywhere. According to rumor, however, some were killed on the travel from the Northlands.

I didn't say it to him when we'd exited the castle after visiting my father, but the sight had surprised me. Who

127

exactly were they? What clan were they with? Human? I didn't get the chance to ask before I was shuffled into the grandest carriage of the line, followed by Leisha, who was also too stunned to speak.

The two of us soon gave up any attempts at conversation. Though the carriage grand, the heavily rutted road and breakneck speed we were traveling at caused it to dip and sway precariously. After a few hours, we were too nauseous to carry on a simple conversation. Leisha, from the last look of her, had turned a peculiar shade of green.

Rhys rode on his magnificent horse with his men when he wasn't scouting ahead in his half-shifted form. I caught glimpses of him now and again outside the small window, and it always amazed me how a jolt of white-hot pleasure sang through my body. I was grateful for the space, which I think he somehow already understood. It made my head ache how fast things had changed, how vastly different my life was in only a few short days.

And most of it had Rhys at the very center.

I wasn't sure how comfortable I was with depending on him, so despite how generous he'd been and how much my body said otherwise, I would do my best to keep some emotional distance, at least for a little while, until I found my footing again.

As though she could read thoughts as well as my mate, Leisha said the first words since we'd started on the second day's ride. "You two look like you've gotten to know each other."

I pressed my warm forehead against the chilled glass of the small window. "I would hope so."

She managed a weak smile. "C'mon," she said with a wince and pressed a hand to her stomach. Her expression was pinched, but she pushed on. "Distract me. What was he like? Are you happy?"

I chewed on my response. "He's… very different than I thought he would be."

Leisha scowled. "Well, that doesn't tell me anything. When I saw you this morning, he couldn't keep his hands off you."

I was sure the blush filling my cheeks was as crimson as the interior of the carriage. "He was surprisingly kind." The blush deepened. "And very generous."

She fanned her face and straightened in her seat. "And?"

My shoulder lifted and settled. "And I don't know. I don't really know him all that well, n-no matter how well we suit in the bedroom."

She sighed. "Well, I suppose if you're with him for a lifetime, at least you're compatible in that department. Before I was a novice at the temple, my parents were going to betroth me to the most loathsome man, so count yourself lucky."

"You were?" I studied her more closely. Three years together and she'd never mentioned it. In fact, she'd hardly talked about herself at all. Feeling like a complete idiot, I reached across the space between us and touched her arm. "You never said anything about it before."

Her eyes went to the window and she was silent for a second. I was about to apologize for being intrusive when she laughed it off and said, "There's nothing to say. I'd *much* rather talk about your betrothed than mine."

We shared a moment of laughter that made me forget all the negative things that had happened to me. In that moment, I wasn't the failed queen who had to be bartered off like chattel to prove her worth. I was just a girl with her friend.

Shivering slightly and heavy with morose thoughts, my spirits lifted when I saw Rhys' draw close to the carriage with his horse. The carriage swayed to a stop without waking the occupants, and Rhys swung down from his horse to open the door.

As he strode across the rutted road, it was as though my body could sense his was near. It lit up like the magicked lanterns townspeople can buy from the capital city markets and send to the skies for festivals around each equinox. Was this the bond? It couldn't be. We barely knew each other.

No matter how much I protested it, there was no denying the way my heart raced. I tugged at the collar of my dress, then scratched where it chafed at the wrists. I'd worn it for its softness, but I wanted nothing more than to tear it off and set it on fire.

Rhys met my eyes as he opened the door and his jaw snapped closed based on something he read in my eyes. Without a word, he held out a hand. After a pause, I placed mine in his, and he tugged me down the steps. I didn't even glance back at Leisha. My brain was too clouded with need for him. It made everything inside of me fuzzy and weak.

He didn't say a word as he pulled me down the line of men and carriages, but I felt as though I could sense his mood as well as I could my own. The awareness of his skin against mine only increased the sense of closeness, of connection. I wanted to pull my hand away, but, for reasons I didn't quite understand or want to delve into, I didn't. It was a silly thing, really, holding hands, but it felt more intimate than making love. So I bit my lip and tried not to let him realized how much I enjoyed his big hand around mine. I didn't let go until he tugged away to open the door to our carriage and help me into it.

I think that's what scared me the most about Rhys. Not that he had the tendency to be fierce and unforgiving like he had the day he murdered the guard who tried to kill me, but that I didn't want to let go.

Rhys settled on the bench seat across from me, his long legs stretched out in front of him and his eyes on me, hot as a brand, though he didn't try to touch me. He barely even needed to the way I was already responding to him.

But he didn't move other than to shuck his overcoat and toss it on the seat next to him. He rolled up his sleeves like it was the middle of the spring season instead of encroaching on winter. Though he didn't need the protection of extra layers like I did, I recalled.

"Rest," he said instead of beckoning me forward, like I wanted, craved, despite my own travel-weariness. "We've got many miles to go yet and you look like you need it."

I wanted to harrumph and shoot him a dirty look, but underneath the want for him was weariness and he was right. We both could use the rest.

"Thank you, I—" I started to say, but then I realized that his mouth hadn't moved. "Did you just…Did I just—"

I pressed a hand to my head to make sure the lack of sleep wasn't causing me to hear voices that weren't there. This mind blending was so odd. The rumble of his chuckle resounded in my head and my eyes snapped up to where he still sat, unmoving. His eyes closed, and head propped against the cushion.

"Don't act so surprised. I told you about the mind blending," he said aloud without opening his eyes. There were deep grooves bracketing his mouth and carved in the space between his brows. The urge to smooth them away was so all-encompassing; I had to twist my fingers into the heavy velvet of the seat cushions.

I tilted my head, considering his words. "Does this mean I'll be able to hear your thoughts, too?" I asked.

"I pray not, but eventually it may be possible." His blue eyes brightened. "Do you want to know what I'm thinking right now?" His voice was silky, intimate, and I was suddenly reminded of the fact we were alone in the small, enclosed space, not that I'd truly forgotten.

"It would probably help to get to know you, considering that we're mated now." I deliberately mistook his meaning. I'd never flirted with another man before, but it was easy with him. "Not to mention that it's freezing, and I'd much rather think about something else. We can't all turn into fire breathers." I pulled my cloak more tightly around my shoulders to ward off the bite of chill in the air and emphasize my point.

"Come here," he said and splayed his legs even wider in blatant invitation.

One I very much wanted to accept. I remembered the warmth of his skin. How satisfying it felt to be in his arms. But the yearning inside of me was so great, it scared me to give into it.

I shook my head. "No, I didn't mean—"

"It'll save us both a lot of time if you just do as I ask,

Elena." His tone brooked no argument. "Now, come here."

Considering the pitiful state of my frozen fingers, despite the many layers I was wearing, I did as he asked and crossed the jolting carriage to his side, practically falling into his arms from weakness. His warmth called to me and I still craved the comfort of his touch. Neither boded well if I was to keep the proverbial distance between us. He opened the placket of buttons at his throat and guided me underneath the voluminous material of his shirt. I groaned aloud, not caring if he heard, as I snuggled into his heat. It felt just as good as I remembered. Better.

He gathered my fingers in his and I watched, speechless, as a brilliant gold glow shined between our clasped hands, melting away the chill. That was new. Rhys chuckled above me and settled my body against his, one of my hands still clasped firmly in his, like it was hard for him to let me go, too.

I supposed there were benefits to being mated to a dragon after all.

"Definite benefits," he said into my hair, his voice hoarse with exhaustion. "But I'm too tired to illuminate them just now, pet, much as I would like to."

His warmth, the cinnamon-smoke scent of him, was too alluring to fight so for a moment I didn't. I laid my head on his chest and allowed him to cradle me like a child as he stroked his hands from my head down to my ice-cold feet, his warmed hands heating me down to the bone.

Half asleep, I nuzzled into his shirt without thinking and his hand stilled on my ankle. "Who are those people?" I asked drowsily. "Your guards. Are they from your clan?"

His other arm rested under my back, cupping my hip and cocooning me against his body. "You have been sheltered, haven't you?"

The comment bristled, but I let it slide because moving away was unthinkable. "I'm sure you know what it's like, at least partially. After," I paused, cleared my throat, "after I learned I couldn't shift, the threat was too great for me to stay at the castle. My brother needed me to go somewhere safe. Not much has happened at the temple in the past hundred or so years and they like to keep it that way."

"My guards are Dragon-Clan."

That caused me to look up at him, my eyebrows in my hairline. "What?" I pressed a hand to his chest as I straightened in surprise. "But I thought they—"

"When the curse befell the Dragon-Clan, it froze them in their human form." His voice grew harsh and the hand on my leg clamped down reflexively. "Now they serve the clan in the only way they can until the day comes when we can break the curse."

I said nothing. I couldn't. I'd never heard of a shifter clan protecting those they deemed weak. Like me. The only reason I was alive was because no one had successfully managed to kill me yet, but they sure kept trying. That and doing so would start a war—one that was probably inevitable. After that, my thoughts turned inward, and I was grateful Rhys left me to them. I chased them around and around until I fell asleep.

The rest of the journey north wasn't pleasant, and I was loath to say it, but it would have been all the worse if Rhys hadn't allowed me the use of his chest for a pillow now and again. A few hours outside of the Corinthine Wood the carriage slowed, jolting me awake from a contented half-sleep against his chest. I blinked up at his face, finding his eyes on me, his expression almost soft in contemplation.

The carriage came to a stop, and I straightened, pulling back the curtains covering the small window. A light dusting of snow covered the ground and the tops of the trees outside—or it would have if there wasn't a regiment of Rhys's clan marching across the road and back up the direction we'd just come from.

Rhys pulled me back down to the seat, though the worry of being so far away from everything I'd ever known turned my stomach to lead. "You should rest."

"Is this where you were attacked?"

His hand came to rest on my back automatically as

we settled back down on the seat. He was quiet a moment before he spoke. In the silence, I tried to read his mind as he could read mine, but there was only silence on the other end. "Yes," he said. "We're a brief journey from where we'll move to the ship."

I closed my eyes and tried to rest as he said, but couldn't shake the feeling of desolation, that hung like chains around my neck, with the increasing distance between myself and the place I had always considered a home.

"Gods, woman, do I need to provide you with a distraction to get any rest?" he asked some time later, the rough tone of his voice startling me from my frenzied thoughts. "Is that the only way you will relax?"

"What kind of distraction?" my mouth asked, before my brain had time to think the question through. His eyes heated and so did my cheeks. "No," I squeaked out, "no, you can't. *We* can't."

"If the last few hours are any indication, I think I most certainly can." He arranged me across his lap as though I was featherlight. I didn't have any time to protest—and I wasn't sure I would have. One second I was blinking up at him and the next I was arranged across his thighs and captured in his powerful embrace.

"Rhysander," I whispered, as his lips mapped the line of my throat. "There are dozens of people right outside that door. We shouldn't."

"Oh, that's the first thing you should learn about me, pet. Denying me something makes me want it all the more. Besides, if either of us are going to get any rest, it seems as though I'm going to have to wear you out first."

He tasted and nipped his way up to my lips, then took them with a commanding sweep of his tongue. I gasped against his mouth, feeling every sensation acutely. From the taste of him—male, a bite of mint, and the hint of mulled wine—to his scent, to the ache low between my legs making itself known again.

His arms caged me against his chest until I couldn't discern where I ended and he began. I opened my eyes, wanting to know if I had the same devastating effect on him as well. A shockwave passed over my nerve endings when we locked eyes. Strangled whimpers came from deep inside my chest, and my hands grappled for a hand-hold in the weighty material of the seat cushion.

The more he used the mental connection between us, the more I recognized his presence in my mind. I could feel it like a thread that connected us, one that vibrated under the pressure of my examination. Was this what happened when couples mated? Did it always happen?

"Relax," he said, *"give in to it. Don't fight it."*

He grinned through our bond and it was like a veil of sunlight washed over me—warm and welcome. I tipped my head up, seeking more, and I felt the responding purr from his chest underneath my hands.

"Are you ready for me to show you?" he asked, peppering kisses on the apples of my cheeks, the curve of my brow, and the tip of my nose.

The words tangled in my throat with each added press of his lips and, dammit, I let his hand tumble through my skirts and drag up the sensitive skin of my thigh. My eyes rolled back as he shared vivid, enticing images of all those things he'd like to do to me. I didn't pull away from him. In fact, I took his hand where it lay in wait just above my knee and moved it higher.

And for the first time, he was speechless.

The realization made me smile. The sensation was powerful. To have such a man at my whim, under my spell. My lids parted and then widened when I found his eyes had turned liquid again. The shorts of his nails scraped against my legs and a moan slipped out, echoing in the constrained space of the carriage. I gave a fleeting thought to the driver in the little cabin out front, but it was promptly whisked away when Rhys's fingers found the juncture of my thighs.

I gave a whole-body shudder, and he hissed out a breath in response. "Fuck, you're going to need to be still, Elena, or I will have to take you here before we even get to the bloody ship."

Enraptured, I inhaled swiftly. "Can we do that?" I breathed.

His answering growl was cut off by the slash of his

lips over mine. His fingers delved into the material covering my center and found me hot and wanting for him. I didn't know if it was to block out the worries and fear about leaving my home, or if it was the growing connection between us rewiring my brain to want his taste, his touch, *him*, but I found that I couldn't get close enough.

He shifted me until I was straddling his thighs, spread nearly indecently above him. "Open wider, sweet—yes, that's it."

I draped myself over him, fusing our lips again. The friction from the constant motion of the carriage left me weak and breathless. His fingers returned where I needed them most and I was nearly overcome with how much I wanted him. The urges, the need, I'd been trying to deny since he retrieved me from the other carriage swelled up inside me, blotting out everything but the thrumming connection between us.

"*Don't be afraid,*" he said.

"I'm not," but my voice broke around the words, betraying me.

His hand coasted up to my chin, and I leaned into it without thinking about it. "*One day you'll remember that it's impossible to lie to me, Elena. You scream the truth to me with your mind. What are you afraid of?*"

I didn't answer him. I couldn't. Even if he could hear my thoughts, voicing them would only make them a reality. So, I kissed him, resolving to drown out my fears, my doubts, and my frustrations with him instead. Because the harsh reality was, even admitting to myself that I cared for Rhys would make it all too real.

Caring for Rhys was almost as dangerous as the man himself.

12

RHYSANDER

She filled me up, my head was buzzing with her thoughts, my senses consumed by her scent and taste, her softness and her little mewls of pleasure. I'd relegated her to a carriage of her own with her maid out of self-preservation. But now, the careful reasons I'd kept my distance had turned to ash in a blaze of lust. I could have spent the nights wrapped in her instead of tossing and turning alone.

The carriage came to an abrupt stop, rocking us against one another, but I barely noticed. My dragon felt she was close, and he wanted to have her again.

And again.

And again.

For once, he and I were in agreement.

I wrapped a hand around her hips to keep her pinned to

143

me. There was no point; she was an eager flame in my lap, ready to blaze to life. I liked having her pressed flush against me, without a whisper of distance between us. Too soon. It was too soon to have this need for her, but I didn't care.

Physical. It was only physical.

I hadn't been with anyone in… longer than I cared to admit. That was all.

Then she swayed against me with the rhythm of the carriage and I stopped thinking at all.

"He feels so good," I heard her think. *"Stars, why does he have to feel so good?"*

I chuckled and brought my lips to her ear. "I can make you feel even better if you'll let me, but you have to ask nicely."

"Don't toy with me, Rhys," she moaned in protest.

My name on her lips was the sweetest benediction. "I'm not. I'm trying to give you what you want."

She trembled so hard I could hear her teeth chattering. "You're trying to make me beg. A princess never begs."

"There's no princess here. It's only me and my mate, and I want to hear those words from you."

Elena leaned closer, her head dropping until our breath mingled. I ached to be inside her, with her heat constricting around me. Her lips brushed against my ear, and my breath caught in my chest.

Something was wrong. I sensed the change in the air and whatever Elena was about to say died on her lips. I wrapped my arms around her in a vice and braced my legs on the opposite bench seats. There was a riot of sound—horses baying in protest and pain, the shouts of men and battle cries of enemies, the clash of wood against wood before rending into splinters—but I had ears only for Elena.

She wrapped her arms around my waist and pressed her face into my chest. My senses attuned to the conversation around us and in a split second, I shifted to my half-Dragon form, my wings spreading around us as the carriage crumbled into nothing.

"What in Goddess' name was that?" Elena shrieked through her thoughts. She twisted in my arms to look down at the onslaught. Swords clanged and sparked as blood stained the snow red.

"Put me down," Elena ordered as soon as she realized what was happening. "I can't leave them."

"No chance in Slaine," I answered, scanning our surroundings for a safe place to leave her while I went back. My dragon seethed, wanting blood, wanting vengeance. His mate was threatened, and he'd turn bone to ash before he let any harm come to her.

"We have to help them," she shouted above the roaring wind. "We can't abandon them."

"I don't plan to," I said. "I'll find somewhere safe for you to wait and then I'll come back for you."

As I said the words, I spotted an outcropping of rock in the cliffs that led to the docks. The scent of salt and rotting seaweed met my nose. I released Elena, who shoved ineffectually against my chest.

"Take me back, damn you. I won't abandon them." The haze of desire that had brought a flush to her cheeks was now a flush of anger.

I leapt into the wind. "Don't move from this spot until I come for you, Elena, I mean it."

Knowing I had about as much a chance that she would obey as I had to turn into a trout, I flew back to the fray, hoping for once in her life she would obey a command. There were more than twice the number of human attackers this time. I could scent their poisoned swords and wondered if I hadn't been so distracted with Elena if I would have sensed them. Could I have prevented the attack?

Swooping in from above, I took out human after human with my bare claws until the blood lust had me thick in its clutches. A roar filled my ears, consuming me. All I knew was the scent of blood and the rending of flesh.

My nostrils flared from the overwhelming reek of the poison: dragon's bane. One slice from a sword would have a Dragon-Clansman at death's door, with no hope of a cure from the poisoned blood that would take them from the inside out. They'd learned they couldn't best us with weapons alone, so this time they were going to make sure to take as many of my people down with them as possible.

Even as I was in the throes of battle, I knew what that meant. They knew we were coming and had been waiting for us.

I saw one, two three, of my clansmen go down with daggers protruding from their torsos by the end. Their bodies lay, barely breathing, amongst our faceless attackers.

One of my clansmen, Berrick, stepped to my side and wiped a forearm over his face. "It seems a waste."

"What does?" I asked through heaving breaths.

"They know they're no match for us, let alone you. Why attack us this way if they know they're going to die?"

"Let's not stick around to find out. Gather the men and the wounded. I must find my mate."

"Yes, my lord. What about the humans?" Berrick asked.

I considered ordering them to leave their bodies to rot for carrion, but decided against it. "Load them on a litter. We'll give them to the ocean and have done with it."

"Yes, my lord," he said and turned to relay my orders to the others.

Weariness settled over me. Dragon-Clan blood was precious and finite. We had so little left to lose that any loss was a significant one. The thought of telling the families of the wounded was one I didn't bear to contemplate until we reached the Northlands.

I lifted my sword and summoned Alaric's *mirror*.

He appeared in the small space available on the blade, a miniature version of himself. Noting my expression, his turned serious. "What is it?" he asked. "What's happened?"

"We've been attacked."

"Again?"

I nodded gravely. "This time someone equipped them with dragon's bane, Alaric."

"Were there any casualties?"

"Several. We'll bring them back to the Northlands and we must tell their families."

"I'll have the clergy ready."

"We'll be on the ship by nightfall. The humans must be dealt with, and swiftly, before we lose anymore clansmen."

"Of course."

I ended the *mirror* without another word. Something was wrong here, but I wasn't sure what. Attacks on shifters by mortals weren't unheard of, but two in such a short time period was a rarity. To possess dragon's bane meant they had dealt with casters to mix the appropriate magical ingredients, and humans didn't often mingle with their Immortal counterparts willingly.

Turning toward the cliffs where I'd left Elena, I resolved to ask Alaric what he thought when we were back in the Northlands. No doubt the sense of doom that weighted my steps would lessen once I was back in the mountains. The humans had only learned new ways to assert their freedoms. I wish that were all it was.

My eyes lifted to the horizon, and I saw Elena on the crest of a hill, wind-swept and furious, marching to us. Stars, she was the most magnificent woman I'd ever seen. And she was all mine. The blood lust was still bright inside me, and I yearned to slake all that need for vengeance with her body. My dragon called out for her and I vibrated with urgency as it swelled inside me.

She wouldn't be pleased, but at least she was safe, and that was all that mattered.

A harsh, heavy wind pregnant with the call of the sea and the salt of the waves blew from her direction. With it, the scent of hot, bloody flesh assailed my nose. I frowned. Was she injured? I hurled myself into the air, my wings erupting from my back so quickly it was almost painful. Elena paused, startled by the suddenness of my movement.

She shifted to make room when I grew close and

that's when I saw them. A human staggered up behind her with a wickedly curved dagger in his grip, already poised to slide across Elena's perfect, white throat. The image of her blood staining the mud and melted snow at her feet flashed across my mind.

No.

With a speed even I didn't know I was capable of, I was at her side. Pulling her behind me, the dagger descended and slashed, ripping at my cloak and slicing through my chest and shoulder. I roared out, more in anger that he got so close to my mate than in pain.

My claws whipped out and tore out the human's throat. He bled out within seconds, his life's blood flowing in a river at our feet. I glared at him, wishing I were a gifted caster who could bring him back from Slaine so I could kill him again.

I turned to Elena, who was as white as the snow underneath all the blood. "Are you harmed?" I asked. My vision went white with rage at the thought. This would never happen again, if I had my way. I'd kill anyone who raised a hand to her. Just let them try.

"I'm fine, Rhys. Let's go back to the carriage."

Stumbling toward her, I shook my head. "The carriage was destroyed by their little trap. I should have been more careful."

"Then someone else's carriage," she suggested and wedged herself underneath my shoulder. Hmm, yes I liked that. Maybe when we got back to my castle, I'd keep her close like this for good. It wasn't always that mates lived together, let alone spent most of their time together, unless they were trying for young ones, but I liked the thought of keeping her nearby.

"Trying to get me alone?" I said, attempting to sound seductive. I must have failed, because Elena had eyes only for Berrick, who was loading clansmen onto a litter for transport to the ship.

"Excuse me," she says to him. "Is there an open carriage we can use? Lord Blaque has been injured."

"A private carriage," I interjected, but neither of them listened. Was I the damned Lord or what?

"I believe your companion's carriage was undamaged in the fray, my lady."

"Thank you," she said. "Come, my lord. We must hurry."

"I'm not going anywhere, sweet. We don't need to hurry."

"We do if you don't want to lose that handsome body of yours."

She guided me to the carriage, even though I must be nearly twice her weight. My little mate could be determined when she wanted to be.

She knocked on the door to the carriage. "Leisha, it's me, open up. The battle is over." The door opened and

Elena said, "Help me with him before he loses consciousness. Be quick now."

Some time later, I found myself on the floor of the carriage with my feet sticking out of the door. The two women were crouched on either side of me and the scent of medicinal herbs was strong enough to burn the inside of my nose. I tried to sit up, but impatient hands pressed me back down.

"No, don't move," Elena ordered. I liked it when she was bossy. "You'll pull the stitches before I've finished them."

It was then I noticed the pain. It bit into my shoulder and traveled deep into the bone. The human must have done more damage than I'd thought. I tried to speak, to tell her I was okay, but she pressed her trembling hands to my lips.

"Hush now, and let me concentrate before this wound becomes infected."

"Is it dragon's bane?" I heard her companion ask.

"…don't know for sure," Elena replied. "But the wound is deep, and it's not his only one. Goddess, he shouldn't have left me behind. If he weren't on the edge of death, I'd put him there!"

I wanted to chuckle, but I was weaker than I liked to admit. Alaric, I need Alaric. But I don't have the words to tell her.

Nevertheless, my mate worked tirelessly over me. The

pinch and pull of her fingers cleaning my wound kept me at the edge of awake. Eventually, even the pain faded beneath the blessing of her touch. This was a magick I'd never experienced before. More powerful than the bond, the mark, the blending of minds. Maybe even more powerful than the curse.

I knew it, I thought feverishly.

I must have said it aloud, because Elena pressed a cool cloth to my forehead. "Hush now, and let me work. Rest, but for Goddess' sake, if you die on me, I will raise you from the dead and kill you myself for leaving me on that cliff."

My responding chuckle took what energy remained, so I did as she asked and let the pain take me under.

As her hands worked over me, I felt the essence of her being brush against mine through our connection. I gasped aloud at the sensation. It was like touching light, touching life. More pure than anything I'd ever experienced in this world or beyond.

I wanted to tell her to stop. It was too much. I was unworthy, but I was almost too weak to breathe, let alone open my mouth and form words.

I'd never heard of mates experiencing a connection so deep. Surely it was the pain staining my thoughts, bending reality.

Surely.

13

ELENA

éjà vu flooded me as I worked to mend the wound like I had with the tenant farmer before my life changed. The gash spanned most of his chest and was so deep it swallowed most of my longest finger. The biggest worry was dragon's bane, but I didn't detect the signature astringent scent signifying its presence.

Leisha's hands shook as she passed me supplies. I saw her peer warily out the carriage door at Rhys's men. "Do you think we should leave him and return home?"

I couldn't have heard her right. "What? No. If we do that, he'll bleed out."

She sent me a significant, measuring look. "You mean you *want* to stay mated to… to this beast?"

Muddling through my thoughts with Rhys's blood staining my hands took significant effort. "I wouldn't have consented to be bound to him in the first place if I didn't."

"My lady, I don't mean to be rude, but we could escape now. His men are wounded and in disarray. You could go back into hiding in another temple or go back to your brother. Gideon would help you."

I pressed a hand to my forehead. "Leisha, you aren't making any sense whatsoever. Gideon helped to arrange our binding. It would make no sense for him to undo all that work. Now be quiet and help me staunch the flow of blood."

She bit her tongue, but I could sense the words she left unsaid. I didn't have time to entertain her nonsense, not when Rhys was growing especially pale before my very eyes. Leisha must be frightened by the attack and it was making her say things she didn't mean. She'll feel better when we got to the ship and set sail for the Northlands.

A headache brewed behind my eyes as I tried to focus on the slippery flesh clenched between my fingers in the dying light. Minutes blended together until finally, I released the breath I'd been holding and looked up. Rhys's men gathered around the carriage entrance.

"Will he be all right, my lady?" the one called Berrick asked.

Grimly, I replied, "We'll know if he wakes up."

"Come, my lady," the gruff Berrick said, a rough stubby candle in his hands. "I'll show you to your rooms."

Leisha took my arm, though she knew from the expression on my face I wasn't in the mood for a conversation. I still hadn't forgotten what she'd said about leaving Rhys. When we were settled in the castle, I'd make sure she was okay, but for now, I was frozen, sore, and in dire need of the bathroom.

I squared my shoulders, and we followed Berrick's hulking form down a maze of hallways lit only by the flickering candlelight. After the third identical turn, I gave up trying to discern where we were going and tried to keep from stumbling. It had taken most of the evening to get Rhys to the ship, tend to the other wounded, and all the supplies loaded. By the time we finished, the moon was high in the sky.

Finally, we reached a corridor with many doors on either side and one at the end. Chatter came from one of the open rooms and I peeked inside as we passed to find a bedroom of sorts. Berrick indicated it was for Leisha, who scurried inside and quickly closed the door behind her.

Wearily, I continued behind the hulking form of

Berrick as we delved deeper into the bowels of the ship. I couldn't feel my feet and my hair was falling out of its plait. I hadn't been able to clean my hands of the blood staining them and wished mightily for a warm bath more than anything.

He stopped suddenly and I almost stumbled into him. "These are Lord Blaque's quarters, my lady. Your trunks have already been delivered. If you need anything, I'm three doors down."

"Thank you, Mr. Berrick."

"Just Berrick, my lady."

"Thank you, Berrick."

"There's a pitcher of water for cleanin' up. I'll have a washtub brought down for you at first light."

"What about Rhys?"

Berrick nodded toward the room. "We thought it best he rests where you could watch after him." The knots in my chest loosened. "Is there anything else you need?"

"No, that'll be all. Thank you."

He stepped aside to let me by, but before I could open the door to the room, he said, "We appreciate what you did out there. Healing Lord Blaque."

"It was nothing," I said.

"Just the same. Good night, my lady."

"Good night."

He left, and I hurried to the bedside where Rhys lay

sleeping. The bleeding had stopped and he didn't have a fever, which was a good sign. I never would have thought I'd wish for him to come back to me, but as I knelt by the bed, that's exactly what I did. I never did much praying when I was at the temple, the Goddess never answered them as far as I was concerned, but I found myself murmuring devotions as I clasped Rhys's hands in mine.

He didn't wake, but the words and the ritual eased my nerves. After glancing at his wounds and reapplying a medicinal salve and a fresh bandage, I made use of the attached facilities and then went to the washstand where a pitcher and cloth waited. The water was freezing, but it was fresh and clean.

I stripped myself from the ruined gown and threw it in a bin in the corner. My trunks were by the bed, and I selected a soft white nightgown. Noticing my grimy hands, I went back to the washstand and wet a towel. A gelatinous bar of soap that smelled of things I'd rather not describe stung a little, but it got rid of the blood.

By the time I finished, my eyes ached and the small space beside Rhys was looking extremely comfortable. I returned to his bed and climbed in beside him. Wrapped in warm furs and sheets that whispered with the scent of his skin, I fell into a deep sleep with him at my side.

My nose crinkled at the scent of charred wood and harsh smoke. I coughed and a hand came to my back and rubbed as I came awake, shooting up with the blankets pooling around my waist. My eyes burned, and I struggled to discern the shapes in the shadows. The embers from the small fire in the grate gave little light, but I didn't need any to recognize the large form by my side.

"Rhys?" I managed, my voice hoarse from the coughing fit.

"I didn't mean to wake you."

I blinked owlishly. "No, that's all right. You're awake."

"You seem pleased," he answered from the darkness. His voice was weak with exhaustion, but *he was awake.*

I felt the bed shift under me as he turned to his side to face me. I'd wedged myself between him and the wall so I was well and truly trapped. Even wounded, he was a force to be reckoned with.

"I'm pleased I didn't kill you." My voice caught, and I didn't realize how afraid of losing him I was until that moment.

He moved closer until I could see the unearthly aqua light shining inside in his eyes. A loud purr came from his chest and I felt it through that ineffable connection between us. I could have sworn it was his dragon reaching out to me. It wasn't something I'd ever heard being possible, even between mates. Shifters only spoke to their own clansmen, never to each other's.

"Were you injured?" he asked.

I shook my head. "No, no I'm fine. Does it hurt? I should check your bandage."

"I'm fine."

Swallowing hard, I said, "You did it on purpose."

His hand came to my face, and I found myself turning into his touch. I didn't realize I'd come to need it so much. This was dangerous. He was dangerous. "What's that, pet?"

"You got yourself hurt so I couldn't be mad with you about leaving me behind."

"I wouldn't have been able to focus if you were around. It would have gotten us both killed." His body was pressed against mine, and the last thought in my mind was about wounds.

"I can hold my own," I said. I put my hand on the uninjured side of his chest. "You don't have to protect me all the time."

The humming in his chest transferred to mine, and he crushed me to him. I felt it all the way down between my legs and I shuddered against him.

"That's two times in less than two weeks when someone has tried to kill you, pet. I think the last thing you need is less protecting."

A weighty silence greeted his words, and I didn't need

our bond to feel the tension emanating from him. Despite the dying fire, it heated the room to an uncomfortable temperature. My skin buzzed with energy trapped just beneath the surface.

"You should rest," I said, trying to ignore how much I wanted to do anything but sleep. "We still have a lengthy journey until we reach the Northlands."

He was equal parts terrifying and alluring, like a dare I desperately wanted to indulge. A risk I knew may be my undoing.

His responding smirk was feral, and he clucked his teeth, chastising. I unclenched my fingers, allowing him to pull the furs down. The weight of his gaze traveled down my body like a touch, searing a path with each revealed inch. Despite my resolve, I found myself trembling by the time the furs reached my waist.

"No more rest," he said. "Now lie back for me."

14

RHYSANDER

My shoulder ached, but it was nothing compared to the overwhelming desire, no *need*, to have Elena. To prove, irrevocably, that she was safe, here, *mine*.

Naturally, she ignored my command. My mate was no submissive. Instead, she pushed on my good shoulder and made me lie back for her.

"We have to be careful," she said and straddled my hips. "I wouldn't want to hurt you even more."

My hands went to her waist as her weight settled over me. I groaned, already hard against her heat. "Nothing you do could hurt me, sweet."

"I thought you were dead," she said softly. "I was so afraid he'd cut too deep and I wouldn't be able to save you. I was really scared."

Reaching up, I pulled on the fabric of her nightgown and it slipped down her shoulder to reveal more creamy white skin. She was so beautiful. To Slaine with keeping her at a distance. She belonged with me, at my side. The mere thought of the knife to her throat had me burning with rage.

Whatever the humans were up to, we would get to the bottom of it.

"You're thinking too much," she whispered. "I must not be doing this correctly."

She had no idea. "Perhaps you should remove this," I said and tugged at her nightgown, causing it to slip down her breasts. The material caught on her nipples and I felt sweat bead on my brow, but it wasn't from the fire in the hearth.

"Help me?" she asked, and I hissed out a breath.

My eyes followed the material as I pushed it up her thighs, then over her lifted hips and finally over her head. She wore nothing underneath, her skin glowing in the combination of moonlight coming in from the window and firelight. Shadows danced over her, and so did my hands.

Unashamed, she sat still above me as I looked my fill. I weighed her breasts with my hands, pinching the nipples into rosy buds and causing her to squirm. Urging her forward, I brought one peak to my mouth, flicking the tip until I heard her moan, then I sucked it deep, teasing a little with my teeth. She was begging by the time I finished with the other and I could scent her arousal in the air, I was drunk on it.

Too greedy for finesse, she shoved down my breeches and freed my cock. Taking it into her hands, she brushed the tip against her entrance, wetting it. I could only grit my teeth and fist my hands into the sheets at my side. My muscles quaked with the need to take her.

She spread herself to ease down over the shaft and I swore. There was no sight more erotic than the vision of her easing herself down onto my swollen length. She lifted her hips repeatedly to settle down more fully, getting used to the fit and feel of me inside her. Her lashes fluttered down to kiss her cheeks and her teeth bit into her lower lip.

When I reached up to touch her, she shook her head. "You must stay still," she ordered, a wicked glint in her eye. "I wouldn't want you to hurt yourself."

Letting out a stream of curses, I did as she bade me. *"You'll regret this. When I get you in my bed at the castle, expect a full repayment."*

"I'd expect nothing less," she murmured, distracted by the slick glide as she braced herself with hands on either side of my head and lifted her hips.

It was too much. I couldn't close off the connection between us and I was assailed by her thoughts, flashes of sensation. Emotion battled inside her as she recalled facing the possibility of losing me. Her fractured thoughts volleyed between how good I felt inside her, to how scared she'd been when she thought I would die.

Her pace became a frantic grind as she sought relief —both from the brewing orgasm and the fear. She was sobbing in breaths of steamy air, collapsing on top of me as she worked herself over my cock. Her desperation sucked the breath straight from my lungs. She'd been desperate for me. *Me.*

I gave into the connection, relaxing underneath her, my hands going to her back. The beast inside of me unleashed, turned my fingers into claws and my teeth into fangs. I'd never made love to a woman this way, with my beast taking part in a semi-shifted form, but now I didn't know if I'd ever be able to go back.

My senses sharpened, and through the blending of our minds, our connection, Elena felt it too. She paused, looking up at me and inhaled a quick breath. Noting some change in my face, she lifted a hand to my cheek. My nails bit into her generous rump, and I bared my teeth.

She wasn't frightened by the change. If anything, her cunt clenched around me and I heard her say, *Mine* in her thoughts as clearly as I heard my own. And oh, the beast liked that very much. He wanted her claim. Wanted her to own every part of us, body and soul.

That was the one thing I wasn't willing to give up…

yet. But he was content to take part this way, for now. To feel her through my hands, taste her with my tongue.

"What's happening?" she asked.

I rubbed a claw down her back, squeezed her ass and used my grip to hold her still while I ground up into her. "My dragon wants to play."

Her breath caught. "Is-is that possible?" I caught an image from her thoughts of her mating with my dragon in full form and chuckled. She didn't find the thought unappealing. In fact, she contracted around me.

"Not that way, sweet mate. He wants to take control of my body."

"I-I didn't know you could do that," she said, tipping her hips to meet each of my upward thrusts. "I've never heard of mates being together in-in that way."

She gave me her neck as I swept kisses from her mouth down her throat where her mark was pearly white against her skin. "Most shifters don't like giving up control that way. Allowing their animal form to take hold in bed is as vulnerable as it gets. Well, taking a claim would be a step above that."

My eyes were on her throat. I'd never wanted to give a woman a full claim, a bond so strong it was nigh on unbreakable. A bond that, when broken, was so destructive it could cost the surviving mate their life. Because it was only broken if one of the mates were to die. Elena's thoughts went to her parents, her ailing father.

"Don't worry, Elena. You won't lose me."

"You can't know that." She shook her head when I started to argue. "I don't want to talk about that now. I want you to make me forget, like you did before. Make me feel good, Rhys."

The sound of my name on her tongue swayed me. "Both of us?" I asked. I trembled from the effort to withhold the beast inside of me.

"I trust you," she answered.

Ignoring the twinge in my shoulder, I urged her onto her back, slipping out of her body only for as long as it took me to remove my breeches the rest of the way and climb back on top of her. She accepted me with welcoming arms and I drove into her with a growl.

I shook in the effort to control myself. The last thing I wanted to do was to hurt her, and I wasn't sure what would happen when I unleashed the snarling dragon inside of me. She wrapped her legs around my waist and drew my gaze to hers with a hand on my cheek.

"*I trust you,*" she thought.

I closed my eyes. When I opened them again, it was as though I were observing the scene as a bystander. I was present, but only partially. My hands reached out and softly sifted through Elena's hair. She held perfectly still as my claws flashed in the glinting moonlight.

Scales bloomed on my arms and down my chest. Hesitantly, Elena reached up to touch them, exploring how they felt under their hand. My eyes shuttered, and a rumbling purr vibrated behind my ribs. My scales were sensitive. I'd never liked to be touched this way, but my dragon did. He liked her hands on us.

He showed his appreciation by reaching between us and taking the bundled nerves of her clit between his middle and forefinger. She gasped as his thumb rubbed the engorged flesh. He alternately soothed and tormented until she was shaking.

How he liked seeing her beneath us. Watching her take my cock as he thrust long and deep. She gasped when she realized my cock had changed, too. Its smooth surface was covered in sensitive, spiny but blunt protrusions that massaged at the walls of her cunt on all sides all at once. When her restless legs writhed, he placed them over my shoulders and held them with one hand while he brought his attention back to her clit.

He brought my thumb to her mouth, and she sucked it in, laving it with her tongue. When it was wet and shiny, he brought it back to her clit. She mewled in pleasure.

It was as though I could feel everything, but couldn't do anything. The sweetest kind of torture. I felt her responses with all of my heightened senses. Her thoughts screamed at me, and I felt everything my beast did to her. Heard how much she liked it, how she wanted more and more.

When she clenched around me, my dragon yielded, victorious. I came back to myself and cried out, unsteady as my senses whirled. My dragon only half gave the reins back, merely wanting to share the moment fully.

Elena was sobbing with her release, her hands in my hair, her body wrapped completely around me with abandon.

"Rhys," she said. "I can't…"

"I'm here. I've got you."

She turned blindly I met her mouth with mine, tongues battling as I swallowed back her moans.

As Elena settled into aftershocks, instinct had me wanting to put space between us, but her legs locked around me like tangled vines. I had no words as instinct turned to panic so I couldn't protest, but she didn't let me.

Trembling though she was from exertion, she rolled with me until I was on my back, like she'd done in the beginning. Her eyes met mine, and she began to ride, adjusting until she found a spot that had moans coming from deep inside her chest. All I could do was hold on.

She was wet and warm and tight around me. Not quite steady because she was tired and twitchy from her orgasm, but she knew what felt good and worked herself over me until all my muscles were tense, trying to hold myself back.

There was no holding back from her. She listened to

my breathing, read the spasmodic jerks from my muscles as I grew closer and closer to the edge, and adjusted herself accordingly until her hips were rocking back and forth over me, driving my cock deep inside her with each movement. I tried to distract myself by nibbling on her breasts, which swayed and bounced in front of my face, but it only made it worse. She tasted so good and felt so good. There was no denying it.

I clamped down on her hips with my claws, restricting her movement and she fused her mouth with mine. I was afraid I was drawing blood, bruising her sweet flesh like a tender piece of fruit, but she lapped at my mouth, murmuring sweet words of encouragement.

I needed no encouragement. There was no stopping. I wrapped my arms around her waist as she brought me to the precipice and over. She bewitched the orgasm out of me as I pressed my lips to the mark at her neck, much to the satisfaction of the beast who prowled inside of me.

15

ELENA

The nights aboard the ship became ours.

Rhys healed quickly, more quickly than I'd ever seen any shifter do. He showed his gratitude for taking care of him by splaying me out before him on the furs like a feast and licking at me until he deemed me well satisfied. The only complaint I had was the journey across the sea came to an end much too swiftly for my liking. I enjoyed having Rhys to myself, isolated as we were amongst the group of his men, who left us alone under strict instruction.

Haran was a small village on the southernmost tip of the Northlands. It wasn't navigable by amateurs because of the steep cliffs of rock and ice. Few ventured to the port save for the shifters who called the frozen continent home. From my vantage point at the bow of the ship, I studied

173

the treacherous approach with more than a hint of disbelief. No one could maneuver the jagged rock without the gift of flight, but somehow the industrious captain angled the boat with a deftness akin to magick. I wondered if the skill was characteristic of the Dragon-Clan.

"Better hold on tight, Lady Blaque," Rhys murmured and wrapped his arms around me from behind. "Wouldn't want you to fall over."

I glanced down over the edge of the ship to the dark, glacial water below. Was it my imagination or were there shadows the size of small carriages shifting underneath us? It was a strange unfamiliar world I was traveling to. The thought was exhilarating. The novices and the temple felt very far away from this foreign land. Rhys pulled my attention from the water and pointed to something in the distance. Peaks of winter white thrust against the clear, blue sky.

"Is that your home?" I wondered aloud. Or maybe I thought it.

"Ancestral palace to the Dragon-Clan. A short ride from Haran."

"I'm eager to see it." I was, truth be told. Something had happened on our journey north I couldn't put into words. A shifting of heart, maybe. I'd had his blood on my hands. The threat of losing him had bound us together more thoroughly than magick ever could.

I let him hold me until the ship docked and his soldiers disembarked. His hand was on my arm as he led me down the rough-hewn wooden planks where another carriage was waiting in the slush-brown snow.

Leisha climbed inside when Rhys took my arm. I turned back to him with a quizzical expression.

"You aren't riding in the carriage," he said with a mischievous grin.

"I'm not?"

"We're going to fly."

My responding smile was automatic. "We are?"

I'd been too afraid after our binding ceremony to enjoy our first flight together. It was considered taboo for shifters to fly with those who weren't their mates, so I could never ask Gideon to take me to the skies. I was certain he'd say no, anyway.

"Would you like that?" he asked softly.

Rhys with a softer side. Who would have thought? "I would. When do we leave?" I couldn't mask the excitement in my voice or the bounce in my step.

Rhys chuckled and pulled me close to his side. "As soon as the men leave."

It took a good portion of the day for the ship to be unloaded, the supplies distributed to the new carriages with fresh horses from the clansmen in Haran. Leisha kept her distance from everyone, not daring to set foot outside. I decided to give her space until we could talk alone. It had been a trying journey for everyone.

"How will this work?" I asked warily, as we moved from the trails to an empty plain. We'd only flown short distances so far.

He led me to the center of the plain and turned to face me, my hands in his. "You'll ride me, of course."

The responding flush in my cheeks, despite everything we'd done, made him kiss me, long and deep. I felt the energy of his dragon in his kiss, the raw power and possession. I wasn't bound to Rhys alone, but to his dragon as well.

Rhys pulled back and turned, motioning for me to place my hands on his shoulders. I did as he instructed, nerves and excitement jangling in my belly. The scales appeared again, but they solidified and thickened, no longer the same texture as his skin. If I weren't watching him with my own eyes, I wouldn't have believed it. His muscles swelled and changed until he was seven feet tall, eight, ten, then fifteen, twenty.

Finally, I sat between the shoulder joints, a dizzying distance from the ground. His muscular body, as blue as his eyes, bunched and twitched beneath me. I could feel his breath and heartbeat thudding through my own, like we were one organism.

"Hold on," he ordered.

"To what?" I screeched.

My scream of terrified delight filled the air, then was swallowed by the whoosh of wind as Rhys's powerful legs launched us skyward. I wedged my knees into the crevice above his shoulder joint and gripped two spiny protrusions on his neck like reins.

The ground flew away as we glided into the clouds. Exhilaration pumped through my body, making me feel as though I were lit from the inside out with Rhys' everlasting fire.

I was flying. I laughed aloud, lifting my hands into the air. *I was flying!*

Rhys dove and I squealed, holding on to the spiny horns. It was freezing so far aloft, but I didn't care. I never thought I'd get to experience flight in my lifetime. It was a secret dream I didn't dare express to anyone, other than myself in my most desperate times. I'd watch the children in the capital testing their wings when I was young, and bitterness would overwhelm me. I'd never be like them. It hadn't been fair to a little girl who had been so different already.

The view stole away any lingering sadness. From atop Rhys's back, I could see *everything*. It was magickal. The patchwork of landscape displayed tiny farms and splotches of ponds and lakes. Ribbons of rivers ran out to meet the ocean. Ahead were the powdered peaks of Rhys's castle. My new home.

When I began to shiver, Rhys' large head turned to

me and his eyes roamed over my body. Except, this crea-ture was his dragon, wasn't it? What a strange feeling to know he'd been with us when we... well... The dragon quaked beneath me and I realized he must be laughing. I frowned at him, and he turned forward. Then his scales began to warm, much like Rhys's had that first night when we met. With the heat coming from his body, the frigid temperature didn't seem so awful, making the rest of the flight pleasant.

I only got nervous when Rhys descended from the clouds. The insignificant dots I observed moving around from above became carriages, and people, and livestock. The peaks, which had been the size of my hand, now filled my entire field of vision. They were magnificent.

Nestled in the center of the mountain range was an ancient castle. My heart leapt in my chest. This was Rhys's home. Our home now, I supposed. The structure rose from the mountain itself, its southern face carved from the stone. It must have taken hundreds, if not thousands, of years to make, considering the striking level of detail. The castle spanned the length of the lower range, turrets protruding from everywhere, reminding me of the spiny "reins" in my hands.

Rhys aimed, not for the grand entrance with doors twice the height of his dragon, but for the uppermost turret. The turret had an opening about thirty feet high with another identical opening on the other side. I realized, as we grew closer, it must have acted as a landing point for the Dragon-Clan, when they were all able to shift into their dragon form. Now, there was only Rhys, who landed in the turret with lithe grace.

He kneeled, his muscles bunching underneath me, and allowed me to climb down from his shoulders. I already missed the skies. When I was on my feet again, which felt odd after flying for so long, Rhys stood, extending to his full height in front of me. I'd never seen a dragon up close before, and Rhys in his full dragon form was awe-inspiring.

I stared at him for a long while, studying. His tail curled around me, pulling me closer. I made an inarticulate sound and held on to it where I could so I didn't fall. It was nearly as long as he was tall and rippled in every shade of blue imaginable. The underside was like burnished gold, glinting in the sunlight. Once I was close enough, his tail rested around me, protective and demanding at the same time. The foot-long spines at the end winked and hissed as they scraped against the stone.

Gathering my courage, I took a step forward and touched one of his back feet. It was tipped with vicious claws in the same burnished gold. I imagined them cutting through flesh like the edge of a razor. His haunches were thickly scaled on the outside, and leather-soft with a fine coating of light gold fur-covered scales. I reached out a hand and touched them. It reminded me of moss clinging to stone. The gilded fur and scales covered him from groin to neck.

What was most impressive were his wings. I gestured with my arms, and he spread them out wide for me to admire. They spanned the entire area from archway to archway. The webbing was the lightest blue, almost white, and was attached to massive spines to bear the weight. At each joint, there were bony talons and more on the entire bottom section of his wings.

His arms were as powerfully muscled as the rest of him and his clawed hands were wicked sharp. Atop his head, rising out from behind curved, pointed ears were two long horns the same gold as the spines on the tip of his wings and tail. I studied his face, searching for some semblance of the man who was my mate. As I did, his eyes narrowed and he bared his teeth in a smile that was more of a grimace, making me laugh.

There he was. My mate.

I gestured for him to come closer and he crouched again. Reaching up, I caught one of his hands that was easily twice my size. He let me climb into his palm, where I sat. Carefully, Rhys brought me up to his face, and I tried not to look down.

Everything about him exuded danger. His canines

were menacingly sharp, visible from underneath his wide grin. Smoke unfurled from his nose in streams of grayish-white with every breath. In his full shifted form, it was no wonder humans and shifters alike were afraid of the mere whisper of his name.

He was power and magick and immortality all in one being.

And he was mine.

Reaching up, I laid a hand on his snout, tentatively at first. He stilled underneath my touch, ears flattening against his skull in submission. Submission to me. This powerful creature, submitting to me. My hand caressed his scales with reverence. The connection between us began to thrum. I swore I could almost hear it out loud.

Heat speared into me when I met his eyes. It didn't make sense, but I wanted him. Blue eyes turned molten.

"*Don't be scared,*" he said into my mind.

"Why would I be scared?" I asked. He didn't frighten me anymore.

Then, he shifted back to his human form gradually and rapidly all at once. His hand jerked and closed around me. I yelped as I fell to my rear. The dragon in front of me shrank, wings and tail retracting. When he was about twice as large as a human, his features blurred, smoothing and reshaping until Rhys's face was staring back at me. As he shifted, I slid down his hand, grasped firmly in his arms, until I was standing in front of him with my hands on his chest.

I looked up into his eyes and smiled. There weren't words to communicate my gratitude, so I reached up and kissed him.

16
RHYSANDER

This wasn't supposed to happen.

She wasn't supposed to care for me. And there was no denying it. I could feel what she was feeling through the blending of our minds. We were only supposed to be together long enough to break the curse and make a son. I'd never planned for emotions to be involved.

I tried to reason through it, apply cold, hard logic, but her mouth was pure chaos. Her hands on my dragon were my undoing. He was anything but logical, ruling the bestial, wild parts of me, overwhelming my good sense. Goddess help me, but I didn't want to fight her anymore.

Members of my household rarely came up to the aviary, having no use for it other than the view, and even then it was depressing for them. So if I were to flip her skirts up and take her right here, no one would be around to interrupt us. Again, like she could read my mind, she pulled me to an alcove inside the stairwell that lead down to the main levels of the castle.

"Eager, little pet?" I asked as her arms wrapped around my shoulders and she pressed herself to me. She trembled. My senses were still highly attuned to her and my dragon was wishing he'd never let me shift back.

"Yes," she said plainly. I could smell her cunt. I bet if I reached underneath her dress she'd already be wet for me.

I threw my senses out to see if anyone was near, and we were alone. At least for a while. The men were hours away and the others would know not to disturb two new mates.

"Turn around." My voice was harsh with need. The scent of her was driving me mad.

She did as I instructed and my breath came out in a hiss full of steam and smoke. Without my instruction, she gripped the skirts of her dress and drew them up over her hips. My claws shredded her sweet little underthings. I didn't care. I'd replace them.

Her breath hitched as I pinned her to the wall. I considered for half a heartbeat if I was being too rough with her. Up to now our bed play had been gentle to an extent, but when I parted the scraps of material to caress her thighs, she lifted her ass to me, beckoning me with the sway of her hips.

"Now," she pleaded. "Rhys, now."

I meant to be gentle, meant to woo her with touches and draw her slowly to completion, but when I pulled my cock free of my breeches and lined it up with her opening, she reached a hand back to grip me. The groan that exploded from my chest was more of a growl, more beast than man.

She stoked up and down my length and I had to press my head hard against the stone wall in front of me to keep from spilling myself all over her hand. Arching, she fit the head of my cock to her sweet, wet cunt and eased herself back. Fuck, how I liked when she took control like she was the master of the beast inside me.

Her head fell back against my shoulder at the first thrust and she balanced herself with hands against the wall. I'd like to say I seduced her, made it last, and made her scream, but I could only say one with good conscience. It was wild. It was violent. It was dangerous. I was no better than the animals in the forests, fucking her with a savagery that she matched and invoked in equal measure.

I ripped the bodice of her gown to reach her breasts, needing to fill my hands with her curves. She made a sound of objection, then I felt her mind cloud with plea-sure as I captured her nipples between my forefingers, tweaking and rubbing them with relentless focus until her hips were rocking back and forth over my cock. Our grunts filled the little alcove, along with the sound of my cock driving into her wetness and her little pleas.

If I had been planning to keep my dragon from wanting a piece of her, too, he had other ideas. When she felt my skin shift into scales, I could have sworn her heat clenched around me. I tried to control it, tried to bring him back under control.

She gripped the hand covering her breast. "What are you doing?"

"Give me a moment."

"What's wrong?" she asked.

I laughed a little. "It seems I have little control where you're concerned."

Her hips ground against me, pulling a groan from my throat. "I don't want you to have any control."

"Keep teasing like that, woman, and I'll make you regret your words."

"I'm not afraid of you, Rhys. I'm not afraid of him either." She tried to reach through the connection like I did when I wanted to tease or talk to her and failed. She blew out a breath. "I don't want you to hold back. I want all of *both* of you. Tell your dragon to come out and play."

She would be the death of us, I decided. I let loose of my control, pinned her completely against the wall and let my dragon fuck her until she screamed her pretty little throat raw for the both of us.

ELENA SMILED RUEFULLY. "What are we going to do about this?" she asked, her voice raw and throaty. I liked it too much to feel sorry. Or maybe I was simply an unrepentant bastard. The animal inside me liked having her wear our mark, liked having her covered in our scent, and walking like she'd been claimed good and hard.

There was no putting her dress to rights. What was left of it would smell of sex, even to the least trained nose. I shed my cloak and wrapped it around her shoulders. I couldn't resist kissing her plump lips again.

"I'll summon a servant to get you a dress to wear until the carriages arrive with your things." With her hand on my arm and her other holding the coat closed around her, I moved to the stairwell.

I didn't want to be concerned, but I was. That didn't mean I had to let her know. Skimming her mind with mine, I let her stream of thoughts wash over me as we made the long trek down to the main floors, passing living quarters, guest quarters, entertaining quarters, servants quarters, and more. Every time we needed a new room, we simply dug deeper into the mountain to suit our needs.

Is it wrong that I'm already thinking about having him again?

I wonder where his rooms are.

Goddess, these stairs go on forever.

My thighs are killing me.

I miss my father already. I wish he were here.

I wonder what his family is like?

Her thoughts blended together, feeling them flow down the connection and fill me with inner light, inner peace. I hadn't felt either in so long, *so long* I welcomed them as much as I was afraid of them. I feared I'd also come to crave them when and if they were ever gone.

We came to the lower floors and a door, which would lead out into a main hall where I could flag down a servant. "Wait here," I told her.

"Where are we?" she asked, peering through the crack in the door when I opened it.

"This is the guest floor. It's less traveled, but I'll be able to find a servant for some clothes. If we go any farther down, we're likely to run into someone else on the stairway before you're dressed."

She clutched at the cloak. "Do I get the tour once I'm presentable?" she asked.

"Only if they end in my private rooms," I answered.

I slipped out into the hall and strode to the washrooms where the linens and cleaning supplies were kept to maintain the rooms, even though very few people visited the castle these days. There, I found Merry, one of the maids who had been with the Blaque family for many years longer than I'd been alive.

"Lord Blaque! We didn't know you were back." Merry was as much a mother figure to me as if she'd been the one who'd birthed me. "Come, we must get you something to eat."

Merry solved every problem with food. From boils to broken bones. She wouldn't be satisfied until everyone around her was as round and pink-cheeked as she was.

"No thank you, Merry. I'm here with my mate, Princess Elena. I'm afraid we've had some... troubles during our journey and her clothes were ruined." I leaned in closer. "She doesn't want to meet the castle in such a state."

Her blue eyes twinkled with feminine knowledge. "Oh, I'll bet they were ruined. Where is she? I'll deliver them to her."

"I'd rather do it, thank you, Merry. I'll wait here for you to return."

"Yes, Lord Blaque. I'll return in a jiff."

I waited for her by the supply closet with the scent of lemonfruit juice and candle wax wafting through the air. Underneath was the slightly damp scent of stone and earth so characteristic of the mountain. Home. I'd just had her, but already I wanted Elena again. I wanted her spread on the bed, *my* bed in this castle. By stars, I wanted to claim her as mine like I'd never wanted anything in my life.

Pressing a hand to my head, I waited for the feeling to pass, but it didn't. The bond between us, the thread that connected us after the binding ceremony felt stronger than ever. Moored in bloodshed and sex, it had strengthened since we left Aurelia, despite my best efforts otherwise. It was like a link in my navel, my heart, my cock, and my head had fused and connected me to her, always. Even this far away, I could feel her, sense her in a way I never had before, not even to my former mate. With her, the connection had been more like an abyss, something for me to drown all the best parts of me in.

"Are you all right, Rhysand?" Merry asked, her hands full of lace and silk. She was the only one left of those who raised me to call me Rhysand.

"Yes, Merry. Thank you for this. If you'll inform Alaric that we're back, Elena and I will meet him in the study."

"What about Soren?"

I frowned, momentarily distracted. "What about him?"

"He's been in a mood ever since you left. Frankly, we've all come close to running him through with something or another. Pardon, my lord. He requested," she said through gritted teeth, "that you speak with him upon your return."

Waving a hand, I said, "Fine, invite him to the study as well." I didn't have time to dwell on our resident misfit vampire prince.

"Of course, my lord, right away."

"Thank you, Merry."

I followed the tug on the link between us, my feet taking me to her without conscious thought. Elena looked up as I reentered the stairwell with the garments in hand. Her own palms were at her stomach as though she felt the same strengthening in our bond as I did.

"Here," I said, choosing not to comment on the change. If I chose not to acknowledge it, it wouldn't be real. "It's time to meet my clan."

17

ELENA

Dragons were members of the Avian Clan, like my family and I, but they were ancient, more ancient than any other Avian. They'd been ostracized due to their resistance to capital culture, but were coveted for their power and strength and the fact that men ruled their clans instead of women like the rest of Aurelian shifters. Unlike the Avians in the capital, Dragons were steadfast in their loyalty to members of their clan. They didn't backstab, power grab, or try to outmaneuver. No doubt they wouldn't take kindly to me, but there was nothing I could do about that.

I'd faced adversity before and I likely would again. Provided they didn't try to kill me, I would fare better than I had in the castle I hoped.

Rhys watched as I stripped out of his cloak and the

rest of the clothes he'd ruined. Was I mistaken or was that satisfaction I saw in his eyes as I discarded the dress and underclothes in exchange for the borrowed ones? The throbbing connection between us hadn't abated like I thought it would after our fevered coupling in the aviary. It pulsed as though our lovemaking had intensified it. An ouroboros of desire. The more we fed it, the more hungry it became.

Once I finished, he took my hand and pulled me out into the hall. Everything about it was grand and worn slightly as things did when they had been well used, but well made. The stone floors were soft with use and the great ceilings softly cream with age. Sconces magicked with flame flickered, turning us to shadow as Rhys led me down the hall to a grand staircase that fed several of the main levels, emptying out into the center of the castle itself.

Everyone stared.

Rhys either didn't notice, or didn't pay attention to the gawking as we traveled down the main staircase. My cheeks must have been blood red by the time we finally reached the first floor. I was meeting his people in a borrowed dress with aftershocks still running through my system. Maybe Rhys had the right attitude. He wouldn't care. Maybe I shouldn't either.

I was still a princess, and I'd be damned if I let anyone else make me feel like less than what I was due.

I'd done that enough my entire life, from the Council to the temple. Even in my relationship with Gideon, now that I thought about it. He'd always looked at me like I never quite lived up to his expectations.

Well, no more.

I wasn't going to be ashamed to be by my mate's side. He'd given me every reason to be proud to be his, and I wanted his people to know I accepted him with my full being, if not quite yet, with my heart. The heart in question was in my throat as he pulled me into a cavernous room.

I noticed nothing other than the books from floor-to-ceiling. I'd never seen anything like it, not even at the temple, which had a room full of religious texts that only the priests read. I'd never had much time for reading, preferring to be outside making mischief or working later when I lived at the temple. In fact, this room reminded me a lot of the temple. There was a mystical, reverent quality to it that made me want to worship.

Rhys let go of my hand and moved into the room, but I was too busy turning in circles, gaping at my surroundings. The shelves were a burnt umber, a deep, rich brown with red undertones and a glossy coating. There had to be dozens of shelves all the way up to the cathedral ceiling. They stationed ladders on rails on each wall for easy access. Jewel-colored glass speckled some shelves. Decorations, maybe? I itched to take a closer look, to explore the volume and discover why Rhys felt they were important enough to collect.

I felt you could learn a lot about someone based on the books that lined their libraries. Were they dry tomes about history and philosophy? Or were they drama-filled fantastical stories with delicate illustrations? I'd have to sneak down here one day and find out.

Catching myself inching toward the closest shelf, I pulled back the hand that had already risen up to snatch a book and glanced around guiltily. My breath caught when I realized we weren't alone. There were two men standing at Rhys' side.

To his right was a man so beautiful it hurt to look at him. Hair the color of fine-spun gold, eyes as green as emeralds, and ears which curved delicately upward. Those eyes danced with amusement, as though someone had told a particularly funny riddle. But it was the faintly purple incandescent rune tattoos on his hands that gave away his immortality. He was one of the fair folk. A faerie. What was a faerie doing in the Northlands? It was rare, very rare, to see one outside The Vale.

If I was surprised at the Fae, one glance at the other man to Rhys' left took the strength right out of my legs and struck fear into my heart. He hadn't bothered to stand from the lush, velvet seat where he sprawled elegantly. One hand toyed with a deadly dagger and the other rested on his thigh, one black-tipped nail tapping out a rhythm as he smirked at me. But it wasn't the dagger or the black striations that spider-webbed across his skin that scared me. It was his eyes. Blood red and gleaming, they bored into me as though he could see through my skin to the life-giving blood underneath. The vampire licked his lips as though he could read my mind.

A dragon, a fae, and a vampire sounded like the beginning to a very bad joke, but there was nothing funny about having the three of them in the same room.

Rhys crossed to me and wrapped a hand around my waist. With him by my side, I was able to move closer to the two imposing men. Recalling my vow to remember who I was, I straightened my spine and looked from one to the other, not shying away from meeting their eyes.

"Elena, I'd like you to meet Soren… an acquaintance, and Alaric, my second-in-command." He placed a hand on the blond fae's shoulder and squeezed. Alaric gave me a gentle smile as though to say he were harmless. "If you have any concern, he's the one you should go to." I noticed he didn't say I should go to Soren.

"Lovely to meet you," I said and tilted my head. The questions I burned to ask were on the tip of my tongue.

"You as well, Lady Blaque."

"Yes, yes, all good and lovely," Soren said with an acid drawl. "I've come as you instructed, like a good little pet, now I'd like my dinner. Warm this time, if you please. If I can't have it from the source, you could at least make certain it's not the same temperature as your precious ice river."

Dinner? I shivered. He meant blood. Where did they get it? Not from people, I hoped.

"Relax, sweet. He feeds from animals while he's here."

"Soren," Rhys said to the insouciant vampire, ignoring his demands. "I'd like to introduce you to my mate, Princess Elena."

"Unless you've brought her as a snack, I don't give a damn."

"Ignore him, Elena," Alaric drawled. "He gets cranky when he hasn't eaten. Or when he has. Truth be told, he's cranky more often than not."

"You would be too if you were being kept against your will. Not all of us are *royalty*." For a moment, I thought he was talking about me, but his eyes were on Alaric.

Royalty? What did that mean?

Before I can ask, Rhys said to me, "Soren was caught feeding on our people—"

"Like the parasite he is," Alaric mumbled, to which Soren bared his sharpened canines.

There were vampires who traveled outside of Erebus, their territory? Everything was changing. Humans were attacking Immortals. Fae and vampires were migrating outside of their territory. I couldn't discern if Acasia was changing for the better… or for the worse.

Naturally reading my thoughts, the oaf, Rhys added, "Soren is finishing up a five-term sentence as one of our spies. One for each life he took."

I turned to Rhys with an amused glance. "You have spies? Why?"

"I like to keep abreast of the goings-on," he answered with frustrating vagueness. I wished I could read his mind, too.

Soren snapped his fingers and shook back his too-long ebony hair. "Dinner," he ordered, then gritted his teeth together. "Please."

"In the kitchens," Rhys answered.

Soren got easily to his feet. There was an animal grace about his movements, almost feline, as he ambled out of the library. He couldn't shift into a bat like ancient myths, but the demons that infected the vampire race may as well have been animals, only they possessed the worst characteristics of us all. Dark, soulless creatures, all they cared about was feeding their appetites. Lust, power, sex. They could never have enough. Without morals or ethics, they took what they wanted without remorse.

"Are you sure it's safe to have him around?"

I knew Rhys would be listening. I smiled a little when I heard, *"We forced him to do a blood pact. He can't feed on anyone or leave the castle without my approval until his terms are up. You're safe here, I promise you. I won't let anything happen to you.*"

He lifted my chin for a kiss. "I promise," he said out loud.

"All right," I said.

"I have to meet with my men, they should be here soon, but Alaric would be happy to give you a tour of the castle."

I experience a flash of dismay, but it passed quickly. I couldn't be with Rhys in our little bubble forever, much as I'd enjoyed it.

"Of course," I said and kissed his cheek. "I'll see you later?"

"I'll be back in time for dinner." After one last hand brushed over my hair, he was gone.

I turned to Alaric, who didn't alarm me quite as viscerally as Soren, but that was the allure of the fae. If vampires were demons, the fae were angelic. Except not as pure of heart. Fae were devious. They loved to play tricks and delighted in always having the upper hand. If Rhys left me with Alaric, he must trust him. Truth-be-told, his golden good looks made me want to be at ease, but I made myself remember you could never drop your guard around a faerie.

"I'd tell you that you have nothing to fear from me, but we both know you're going to be on your guard, so I'll refrain. Instead, why don't I show you the castle and you can ask me anything you want to know about Rhys?"

I was too intrigued to be cautious. "Really?" I asked, and followed him out again with one last glance as the library. I couldn't wait to go back and explore when I had more time. Considering this was now my home, I supposed I had all the time in the world.

"The castle is organized in levels. The main floors are for meeting areas: the ballroom, dining room, the library, etcetera. Above that are the guest levels, then the living quarters. When we're finished with the tour, I'll show you to Rhysander's room."

So we would be sharing rooms. Interesting. I knew some mates didn't. As I pondered what that meant, Alaric gave me a tour of the main floor from the elaborate ballroom to the dining room with the biggest fireplace I'd ever seen and a table big enough to fit nearly fifty people. My favorite place after the library, though, was the greenhouse and lush gardens. I didn't think there'd be a garden since we were so far north and as far as I knew, it was nearly always cold. Magick must keep the beautiful blooms alive.

Alaric led me through the garden, humoring my questions, as I studied each bloom. It reminded me of the gardens I used to tend at the temple, which felt so far away now. So much had changed.

"He has no family left. His father went on to be with

the Goddess a long time ago and his mother died in childbirth. There were no other children," Alaric said, when I asked about Rhys' family.

So we were alike in that regard. I wonder if that's why he agreed to help me with my father.

"How many clansmen live here?" I asked to distract myself from images of little ones who had Rhys' eyes and baby dragon wings. Goddess help me, but the image made my stomach turn to mush.

"Most of the Dragon-Clan live in the city and a good portion work here in the castle. There aren't as many left so Rhys likes to keep them close."

I bent to sniff a red rose which bloomed from a bush nearly as tall as I was that grew from a chunk of ice. "Incredible," I whispered. "They must be an extraordinary clan to come together during such strife."

"As close as I've ever seen."

Straightening, I turned to Alaric and tilted my shoulder. "How do you know Rhys? I'll admit, I've never met a fae outside of their own territory, so I'm curious. Are you under punishment like Soren?" Somehow, I didn't think so. Alaric didn't give away much, but from our brief interaction, I didn't get the impression he would give in so easily. Behind the congenial facade was a calculating man. I had no doubt he observed me for any faults or areas of weakness.

He could observe all he liked. There would be no weakness as far as he and Soren were concerned.

Alaric led me to a garden bench and gestured for me to sit. "Rhys is a smart man, smarter than many give him credit for. He found me near death one day during his travels. He saved my life in exchange for my fealty to him. I've been with him ever since."

"Forgive me, but it sounds like enslavement."

"No, my lady, on the contrary, a man's word means everything to the fae. He promised to save my life. When he made good on his promise, I made good on mine. Fair's fair."

It never made sense to me how fae could be so wily and so dependable at the same time. I tabled my curiosity on the subject for a later date. I had enough problems to deal with.

"Is there anything else I should know?"

He hesitated. "I would stay away from the crypts underneath the castle, if I were you. Rhys is very protective of them."

"The crypts? What is—"

"Why don't I show you to Rhys's room? He should be finished now and I'm certain you're weary from your journey."

I knew when I was being brushed off, but I didn't argue. Pushing my luck on the first day wasn't wise, but I was sure there would be other opportunities to discover the secrets in the mysterious crypts.

I wondered if it had anything to do with his former mate.

There were still so many things I had yet to learn about Rhys. Before I'd left Aurelia, I'd been certain I didn't care about his past. Our arrangement was business-like and that was fine with me. Then, I'd nearly lost him and I realized, somehow, it had become anything but business.

RHYSANDER

"I t's truly not necessary," Elena protested. She perched at a vanity, brushing out the dark sheet of her hair as I sat on the bed, watching her. I couldn't seem to take my eyes off her.

Alaric had deposited her safely at my door and I wasted no time informing her of a welcome ball we would throw at the castle the following night in her honor. Members of my clan had been waiting lifetimes to see me mated. Or rather, they'd waited lifetimes to see the curse broken. All their hopes were on me, on us. It hadn't occurred to me before, but I wondered if she felt the pressure to save them as I had for so long.

"I can't think of anything more necessary."

Goddess help me, but I wanted to show her off to all my clansmen. Not because I believed she would break the curse or because I wanted her to be the mother of my young, but because of who she was as a person. She was strong and capable. Kind and thoughtful. Truly better than a beast like me deserved.

My dragon wanted to have her on our back and fly her around the Northlands again, like a prize we'd claimed. I compromised with a ball instead. She was lucky I convinced him otherwise because I was starting to think he had more influence over my decisions than I thought where she was concerned.

"But I've only been here one day. I won't know anyone." She bit her lip, worrying the flesh between her teeth.

She was impossible to resist. The bond between us was an ache in my stomach every time I was away from her. After I left her with Alaric, I tried to distract myself with checking on my men once they arrived, then directing where to put our things. The longer I was away from her, the more I needed to see her. I'd never heard of the bond being so strong and I'd certainly never experienced it.

Even now, it tugged at me, pulling me like a hook around my spine, urging me to get closer to her, take her in my arms, and make her mine again. She still smelled of me, but only faintly. The bond urged me to touch her, taste her, take her. It consumed me to the point it was all I thought about.

I shook my head to clear it. "You'll have me. Your Leisha will be there. So will Alaric and Soren."

Elena frowned at me. I had eyes only for those lips. "Alaric, maybe. But I wouldn't consider Soren someone I'd like to know. Leisha has kept to her rooms since she realized there was a vampire in our midst. I think she's scarred for life after the attack."

Chuckling, I said, "He's not too bad once you get to know him, bloodsucking aside. I'm sure she'll settle once she gets used to being here."

"I find that hard to believe. You said you made a blood pact with him? What does that mean? I've never heard of it." Her voice was thick with doubt. I couldn't blame her. Vampires weren't beings I'd recommend trifling with.

Unable to resist any longer, I rose to my feet and crossed to her. Standing behind her at the vanity, I took the brush from her hands and resumed brushing her hair. Smiling faintly in amusement, she began rubbing cream over her face. I'd never been the domestic sort before. My previous mate had preferred to keep separate rooms, and for that I was grateful, but I could get used to this. It was only her first night in my rooms and they felt more like home than they ever had.

"A blood pact binds a vampire to their word. When I found Soren had murdered clansmen, I tracked him down to a cave outside the city. I caught him unawares and roasted him until he was nothing but blackened meat and bones." At Elena's gasp, I added, "It wouldn't kill him. A vampire can only be killed if you remove his heart and destroy it."

"Sounds disgusting," she said.

Nodding, I continued, "He agreed to the blood pact, which involved the exchange of blood between those making the pact, in order to save his own skin. He'll never be able to take another's blood without their explicit consent and he won't be able to leave the Northlands until his terms as my spy are complete."

"Why would you even want him for a spy?"

I set the brush aside and moved her hair until it lay in a sleek waterfall over one shoulder. "Vampires can be useful under certain circumstances. As you know, they're able to coerce their victims so they don't feel any pain during the feeding process."

She shivered. "I'm aware."

"Well, they're also able to use this coercion even when they aren't feeding. It's useful when I need him to get information from a particularly unwilling subject."

"Rhys, I have to say...you keep some interesting company."

"None as interesting as you." Or as beautiful, but it went without saying.

Giving a little laugh and smirking at me through the

mirror, she said, "You're only saying that to get me into bed."

"Now who is reading whose mind?"

"I don't have to be able to read your mind to know what's on it in that regard."

She let me pull her to her feet and toward the bed. Already her heart was beating double time. "Maybe one day you'll be able to read my mind, too."

"How?" she asked.

"For true mates, sharing thoughts happens whenever both mates accept the claiming bond." I fingered my mark on her neck as her eyes went to my own bare skin. "If that were to happen, you could hear and speak to my mind as well."

The thought wasn't as horrifying as I thought it would be.

Which should have sent fear streaking through me.

But it didn't.

Instead, I took her to bed and loved her well into the night. If the walls hadn't been made of the thickest mountain stone, the entire castle would have heard her screams.

EVERY TIME I woke up to her, I liked it a little bit more. She hoarded the covers, liked to sleep with her legs and arms wrapped around me like a snake shifter, and came awake as grumpy as a beleaguered cat, but it amused me more than irritated me now. Which I didn't care to examine too closely.

For the first time since my first mate, Valeria's death, I felt a measure of hope. It was so foreign that when I blinked myself awake and saw Elena sleeping next to me after our first night home; I frowned and rubbed at my chest. There was a tender ache in my heart I didn't know what to do with. Ignoring it seemed wisest.

Instead of dwelling, I pulled Elena closer to my chest. She was sleeping as I learned she always did, with one arm around my waist and one ankle thrown in between my legs. It was as though she was afraid I would sneak away in the middle of the night and she was making sure she woke up if I did. Her hair was a tangled mess, even though she'd brushed it thoroughly the night before. I knew because I liked watching her. It pleased me to make her writhe against the bed as I licked her until she begged me to stop, in part because I knew it meant I'd get to watch her at the vanity again.

She came to slowly as I ran a claw down her spine. Groaning and turning from me, she murmured, "No, I'm not ready."

"You have half the day left to prepare, sweet. Plenty of time to get ready for the ball."

Her eyes popped open. "Half the day? What do you mean half the day until the ball?"

"It's nearly noon, pet. We slept in."

"I don't think I can be ready in five hours. I don't know if I even have a dress appropriate for the ball."

A smile curled at my lips. "You do. I've left it in your dressing room. One of the maids will help you."

"Will you send for Leisha?" She nibbled at her lip. Now I wished I hadn't mentioned the ball. I liked soothing the discontent from her every morning.

"Of course. Your dressing room is through that door." I pointed and added, "I'll have a tray brought to you. I'm sure you'll be hungry."

She gave me a lingering kiss that nearly had me saying fuck the party, and then she was slipping from the bed with one of the thin sheets wrapped around her body. The door closed behind her.

Already, I wanted her back with me.

Music filled my ancestral home like it hadn't in a long time, too long. It echoed through the halls along the stone like a heart being brought back to life. The orchestra brought their song to a close, and all eyes went to the dais, where Elena was standing, unsure. Her maid hovered behind her, her face blank.

But I only had eyes for Elena.

She wore white again, the color of my clan. This dress was a simple column of shimmering fabric. The cutouts at her hips, stomach, sternum, and collarbone both enticed and concerned me. Despite my brutish nature, I'd never been the possessive sort. Until now. The flashes of her skin and glimpses of her shadowy form beneath the layer of fabric were certain to drive me mad by the conclusion of the ball.

She scanned the crowd until her gaze found me. I cast out my thoughts to feel hers. I'd grown used to gauging her emotions without conscious effort. Being without her, even for the short period of time while she got ready, felt like I was missing a part of myself.

"*There he is*," I heard her think. I sensed the wave of relief that washed over her as if it had been my own.

I left Soren and Alaric, who had been conspiring about the human attacks, to climb to where Elena was standing. Her smile as I grew closer was as automatic as mine. I brought her fingers to my lips and felt her shiver.

"You are radiant," I said, voice gruff. It took supreme self-control not to scoop her up and take her back to my rooms. My dragon flapped his metaphorical wings impatiently. Scales glimmered on my hands.

At the sight of my visible struggle for restraint, Elena smiled silkily. "I take you like the dress?"

My hands went to the cutouts at her hips and I let warmth gather in my fingers, causing her to shiver under my touch. Remembering there were a hundred other people in the room, I turned, placing my hand on her back, which I realized was also bare. The attendant announced our names, and I led us to the center of the dance floor as the orchestra sailed into a dreamy tune.

"I like *you* in the dress even more," I said close to her ear. I didn't need to read her thoughts to know she liked it when I whispered to her that way. Her trembling body told me all I needed to know.

"Who are all these people?"

I glanced up from her for the first time. My clansmen were hovering at the edges of the dance floor with pensive expressions. They were as hopeful as I Elena would break the curse, but they were also hesitant to trust another mate for their Lord. Part of me knew how they felt, but the other—the other didn't care if she was going to break the curse or not. I only wanted to live long enough to enjoy her.

"They're your new family," I answered truthfully. They may be hesitant, but the Dragon-Clan was, and always had been, loyal to its people. As my mate, no matter their reservations, they would be loyal to her— family to her—as well.

Her head twisted from side to side as she tried to take in the sheer number of people around us. "*All* of them?"

"All of them."

"I suppose they're all watching to see when we'll add one more, huh?"

Smiling, I said, "Not literally, but yes."

"No pressure."

"At least we'll enjoy trying."

At that she smiled. "Why don't you introduce me to them?"

ELENA

"I want to show you something."

Rhys tugged me toward an empty balcony. The lilting music from the orchestra trailed behind us as he shut the doors to give us privacy. My heart was soaring as high as we had the day before. The girl who had been banished to the temple had been welcomed with open arms by the Dragon-Clan. I felt more at home in their midst after one day that I had throughout my whole life in Aurelia. I wasn't sure how to feel about it, but for now, I was going to enjoy it without reservation.

"What is it?" I asked.

Rhys pulled me to the gardens where Alaric had given me a tour. The hot, sweet scent of flowers tickled my nose. He brought me to a birdbath with a small pool of clear water.

"Rhys? What are we doing?"

At first, I thought he was going to pull me into his arms for a tryst, then when he didn't, I frowned. He lifted his hands and waved them over the water as he chanted words in another language. The surface of the water rippled, and I started to question him again when an image moved across top of the water.

"My men and I communicate with a spell we learned from casters that has been passed down for generations. We call it *mirroring*. It allows you to view another through any reflective surface or, in this case water, to see a window into another place. I wanted to prove to you that I remembered my promise to help you with your father. It isn't safe to bring him here with the humans attacking travelers, so this compromise the best I can do for now."

Whatever I had expected, it wasn't this.

As he said, an image of my father appeared over the water, shone through it like a fluid mirror. If I had to guess, I'd say the viewpoint was the very window I'd opened in his rooms the day I'd arrived at the castle. He looked worse than ever. His skin was sunken into his cheeks, his body frail and worn, as though a stiff wind would cause him to disintegrate. Gideon sat at his side, forcing a draft down his throat, murmuring low words of encouragement.

I didn't know when I'd moved closer to the water, but

my hand was gripping the edge so hard my knuckles were bone white. "Oh, Father," I whispered to his reflection.

Rhys wrapped a comforting arm around my waist. "I plan to send Soren out to discern the cause of these attacks and the threats on your life. I believe the two events are linked somehow. As soon as it's safe, I want you to know we'll send for him. I promise you this on my life."

I hadn't even thought of him being attacked. Newfound horror spread through me. What if something happened to him while I was away and couldn't help him?

Rhys pulled me close, until my head was cradled on his chest. His big arms wrapped around me. "*Nothing will happen to him, sweet. He's safe for now at the castle. Despite what you may think, Soren is the best at what he does.*"

That I couldn't deny, but I still ached with impotent anguish. There was nothing I could do for my father when Acasia was too dangerous for him. I would have to trust Rhys when he said he would help. I did trust him. I shouldn't. Every whisper and rumor in the capital warned me away from him, but my mate had been kind to me, and honest. And I wasn't the sort of person who turned their back on an agreement.

"I believe you," I said against the thud of his heart-beat. "I only hate there isn't more I can do for him."

"Tomorrow, you can tell Soren everything you can recall about the attacks, as I have. The more information he has, the easier it will be for him to find those responsible."

"I'll do what I can." Finally, I looked up at him. He was magnificent in breeches and coat the color of smoke. The cut emphasized the broadness of his shoulders and the tapered strength of his hips. "Thank you. I hadn't realized how much I missed them. Thank you for sharing this with me. You didn't have to."

"Yes, I did. You left your only family behind, and though my clan is now yours, I know how much they mean to you, and I'll do whatever it takes to make my mate happy."

I don't know how to explain what happened next. It felt like the essence of me, the part mired in our ethereal connection, reached out to him. I yearned to be as close to him as possible, in every way. It was only supposed to be an arrangement, a deal, a sham, but our bond was becoming more real to me than anything in this world.

My eyes closed, furrowed, as I tried to understand what was happening. The connection between us had only been one way before now. He could read my thoughts, could speak into my head, but never the other way around. Trying to concentrate, I reached my mind out and felt the bond that linked us together, a mixture of the two of us. I traced it back to its origin and felt Rhys, in his purest, most honest form.

Panic threatened. "Rhys?" I whispered.

"I feel it," he said, sounding as flabbergasted as I felt. He was trembling underneath my hands.

"What's happening?" My voice quivered.

"I-I don't know, sweet."

I traced the line of the connection, feeling where it started in the center of my spine and flowed out from my belly across the distance between us. Before it had only been a hint, the feeling of being moored to another physical being. But now...now I could sense Rhys on the other side.

It was indescribable. I couldn't make out his thoughts or speak across the bond into his mind like he could. It was as though I could sense him through a glass wall. Everything on the other side was muffled, but now I could hear it, even if I couldn't understand it.

Reaching out a metaphysical finger, I stroked the glass wall. Rhys shivered around me as though I'd touched *him*. "Wow," I said in awe. "Can you feel that?"

His voice was hoarse when he spoke. "I can feel you. I can see you touching me."

When I opened my eyes, he was gazing down at me, his eyes that striking, otherworldly blue. "Do you think they'd mind if we skipped the rest of our own party?" I asked.

RHYS LEFT EARLY the next morning to meet with Soren and Alaric to discuss Soren's next assignment. I'd already relayed everything about the attacks that I could remember. I peeled myself quite reluctantly from the bed, but decided I should track down Leisha to see how she was transitioning. So much had happened in so little time. I didn't want her to think I had forgotten her.

After sending word with Merry, who I'd come to love in the short period of time since I'd been at the castle, I dressed and ate a small breakfast of fruit, toast, and lemonfruit juice. By the time I finished, Leisha returned a note by way of Merry saying she'd meet me in the orchard just outside the castle grounds.

I'd heard of the orchards, which had been magicked long ago to bear fruit in the frigid temperatures of the Northlands, so I was eager to see them. I had so much to tell Leisha and couldn't wait to hear what she thought about our intriguing new clansmen.

Those I'd met at the party waved to me as I left the castle. It was so refreshing not to be judged by everyone I met. They knew about my dark secret of course, and they didn't care. It boggled my mind. They saw me as some sort of savior instead of some sort of oddity.

As I ventured into the orchard, I wrapped my cloak more tightly around my shoulders and did my level best to forget about the warmth of Rhys's bed and the comforting crackle of the fire in the background. Much as I wanted to, I couldn't spend *all* day in bed with him.

The thought put a smile on my face. It was a beautiful day and somewhat magickal underneath the full blooming trees. I still worried about my father, and wished I could see my brother, but for the first time in my life I had hope, thanks to Rhys.

I found Leisha a ways into the forest. It was so thick I couldn't see the castle or even the sky overhead. She was sitting at the base of a tree and stood when I came into view.

"Princess, I'm so glad you made it. I was worried they wouldn't let you come."

"Don't be silly," I said and pulled her into a hug. "I've been meaning to set aside some time to speak with you, but it's been a whirlwind since we left the capital. So much has changed already. I hope you're settling in well. The Dragon-Clan has been so hospitable."

As we walked through the orchard, Leisha seemed to choose her words carefully. "Hospitable, yes. I'm grateful you made time for me. I've been worried for you."

"Worried? Whatever for? I hoped you enjoyed the ball. I thought it was beautiful."

Leisha grabbed my arm, her expression pinched. "My lady, I'm worried because you don't seem to believe you're in any danger. Your mate murdered someone. We were attacked coming here. What makes you think you're safe with him?"

I took Leisha's hand in mine. "I appreciate your concern, but Rhys would never hurt me. Those men who attacked us were human, and the Dragon-Clan is doing everything in their power to find out who orchestrated the ambush. I know you were scared, and you had every right to be, but Rhys won't let anyone harm us. I promise you."

"Is that so?" came a silky voice.

A blade appeared, quick as a lightning strike, and nicked at the underside of my throat. My eyes snapped to the side, and I resisted the urge to swallow. A bead of blood crested on my collarbone and stained the neckline of my dress.

Leisha whimpered in front of me, but I couldn't take my eyes off the brilliant green ones of the fae holding me, didn't dare. My fingers dug into the skirts at my sides, but otherwise, I didn't move for fear of dislodging the blade. Or enraging the smirking Immortal holding it.

The fae leaned forward and scented the air. "We were ever so surprised to find you here, looking like a pair of lost little girls." He laid his cheek against mine and nuzzled as though I were a long-lost friend. "We'd be happy to help you find your way home."

His companions snickered and hissed in agreement. What were they doing in the Northlands so far from their territory?

"Thank you," I managed to say carefully. "But we aren't lost." I let out a relieved breath as the pressure from the blade released, and I could swallow freely.

"That's too bad," he said moving around to face me and pressing the flat of the blade against his lips in contemplation, tapping lazily. "We could really use the company. It's been a long day of traveling and we still have a long way to go."

"Well, we appreciate the offer—"

"Do you?" he said idly, sheathing the blade. "You don't seem very appreciative. Perhaps we should teach you a little lesson in gratitude. You shifters are an ungrateful lot, after all. Taking our land. A thankless bunch. Yes, I think a lesson is what we need here. The question is, which of you two to choose, hmm?"

My stomach clenched and at the same time, my bowels turned watery. The fae were known for their tricks. For twisting words and using mortals and Immortals alike for their amusement. I had never encountered a fae myself before Alaric, and having done so now, I already wished I never had. These fae were nothing like Alaric

"We are most appreciative…"

"Corden." He steepled his fingers, his head cocked to the side as he studied me.

I endeavored to keep my gaze locked on his, my voice calm, but it was a struggle. Fae enchantments, if they're strong enough, can keep a shifter from changing. If they'd already caught Leisha before her shift, then the only way we were going to get out of this alive was by bargaining. And the last thing you ever wanted to do was bargain with a faerie. I had never heard of anyone doing so and getting out alive, but I had to try.

"We are most appreciative, Corden." I bowed my head low.

He stood, and his long-legged form towered over me. So much so, that the thin slice in my neck screamed in protest when I slowly glanced up. Three other fae gathered around him, their too-wide smiles baring wickedly pointed teeth.

"Maybe you need some convincing," Corden said, prowling through the clearing. I followed his lithe form to where Leisha now sat wide-eyed, her arms twisted behind her back by another fae. Fear had bleached her face of its color, and pale streaks of tears painted her cheeks with luminescence.

My heart sank into the roiling pit of my stomach and

I swallowed thickly. Corden snatched Leisha from his companion and urged her in front of him. He thrust her forward, and she tumbled into a heap at my feet with a high-pitched squeak. My heart thudded slowly in my chest and blood rushed in my ears. I inhaled through my nose to try and maintain a sense of calm. I needed my head clear, but panic made it extremely difficult to think.

Our lives would depend on it.

"We'll go with you," I said.

Leisha looked up at me. "No!" she screamed. I gave her a stern look, but she continued to shout it over and over again. One of the other fae grew impatient and kicked Leisha in the stomach with the pointy toe of his boot.

I wrenched to my feet, but Corden was there in a flash, holding my arms behind my back. I managed to swallow my screech of pain and choked out, "Don't hurt her."

"Ah, so you want to bargain," he said, a gleam of anticipation in his eyes. "We could do with some enter-tainment and this one here looks like a lovely little morsel. She may do quite nicely."

"No," I growled, "You may have me. I'll do whatever you want."

Corden slithered next to me, hissing in my ear, pulling me close to his body so his front was pressed against my back. His lips caressed the curve of my shoulder. "Now that sounds delightful." He shoved me away and I tripped over my feet, sending me spiraling into the frozen earth next to Leisha's sobbing form. "Dance for me, girl," Corden said idly, but there was no mistaking the purr of anticipation in his voice, despite how relaxed he seemed.

I got to my feet and the other fae joined Corden in a circle around me. Their magick hung thickly in the air, causing my nose to twitch and the air to warm. My fingers tingled as it made its way through my body.

Faerie circles. I'd heard about them, too. How they made mortals and shifters alike dance, quite literally, to their deaths. They could go on for days, until I was wrought with starvation or dehydration. Until my feet were too bloody to move, and they grew bored, leaving me helpless to die on the ground in the middle of the forest, an exhausted heap of bone and sinew.

I began to dance, swaying my hips, my hands above my head. The moves came to me naturally, more from magick than any kind of talent of my own. My feet counted out the steps, mixing the dirt and snow and making my already frozen feet grow numb inside my inadequate shoes.

One of the fae pulled Leisha from the ground and held her by the jaw, her face turned toward me so she could watch my punishment. Their smiles were even bigger now, stretched across their luminescent faces like horrible masks. As I spun faster and faster they all blurred together until it began to feel more like a dream than reality.

Before long, I lost all feeling in my feet, and for that I was grateful. By last glance they had grown bloody, blisters forming in the places where my shoes rubbed against my heels. I didn't know what would be worse: the pain from the dance, or the frostbite that would surely set in if they made me dance long enough. The orchard was magicked so trees could grow in the snow, so there was still plenty of it on the ground.

At some point, I heard Leisha's sobs and their jeers fade away, too, until all that was left was a pleasant sort of darkness. Sweat coated my skin, even in the cool night air, and I shrunk away from the reminder of where I was and what I was doing and sank into the welcoming darkness.

I realized the exhaustion, the helplessness, was really the undoing of all the unfortunate souls captured by the fae. Once all feeling had been magicked away, once your body grew too weary from the dance, the beckoning call of nothingness felt like the best way out. My ears roared with the rise of unconsciousness, and it caused a smile to spread.

At last.

A delicious heat spread over my entire body, causing

me to groan with the warring feeling of pain and pleasure. Tingles and shocks raced throughout my arms and legs, and most of all, my feet. Oh, stars, my feet. Soon, a fog consumed me.

I sat up with a moan, bedraggled and confused. I winced, putting a hand to my forehead, but that did little to dispel the spinning or the muddle. Blinking, the clearing in the forest came back into view and I had to shake my head, which I immediately regretted, to register what I was seeing.

A magnificent dragon, *my dragon*, crouched in front of me, his teeth bared and licks of flame spewing front his flared nostrils. His spiked tail whipped behind him, keeping two of the four fae at bay as he stared down Corden and his accomplice, the one guarding Leisha.

Despite the gnawing ache in my wounded feet, I scrambled to them, gripping a tree to keep upright. The dragon eyed me for a moment before baring his teeth at Corden.

"You dare come to my land and steal my mate," the dragon seethed. I hadn't even been aware he could speak, though his voice seemed to emanate from the space around us rather than from his mouth.

Warmth that had nothing to do with the flames shooting from his mouth spread throughout my body. *He came for me.*

"Your mate?" Corden said, flicking an accusing glare

at me. "If she's your mate, perhaps you ought to keep a better leash on her. We found them…traveling away from your castle. Seems like you can't quite keep one, can you?"

Rhys growled, spitting flames at a smirking Corden. "Leave. Now, before I reduce you to ash where you stand."

The fae blinked, and then they were gone.

Relief weakened my knees, and I slumped onto a pile of melted snow, the dampness seeping through the material of my dress and cloak, but I didn't care. I hurt everywhere, my escape, such as it was, had been short-lived, but I was alive. For a while there, I hadn't been certain I wanted to.

Rhys landed, shifting back into his human form. He stayed crouched on the ground in front of me, his tan skin luminous even in the pale light from the splintered moon. His chest heaved as he got to his feet and I didn't need to see his face to know that his eyes were glowing bright red. When he reached for me, I couldn't move, I was so numb with pain and a bone-deep tiredness.

"Can you move?" he asked quietly.

"I don't know," I said. "Is Leisha okay?"

"Yes. I'll take you both back to the castle. We wouldn't want to be here if they decided to come back."

He paused helping Leisha climb onto his back. He

was going to carry me in his arms once he shifted back to his dragon form since I couldn't walk.

"What's wrong?" I asked.

His eyes shuttered, and he whispered too soft to hear. I pulled my hands from around his waist and it's then I noticed the blood.

The sound of galloping horses and war cries pierced my exhaustion and shock. They were close, not so much that I could see them through the trees, just enough to know if he didn't get us out of here, we'd both be dead.

"We can't be that far from the castle," I told Rhys. "Can you fly?"

"You should go," he said. He spat blood onto the snow. My fingers stilled on his arm and he started to slide down. I hefted his weight back up and he smiled morosely, blood smeared across his lips. "Dragon's bane," he whispered.

Our pursuers weren't the fae, coming to finish us off.

They were humans. The same men who'd attacked us in Braeden. The same humans who had already tried to kill Rhys.

The ones who'd just shot him with a poison-tipped arrow.

2 0

RHYSANDER

Another arrow cut through the air, grazing the fleshy part of Elena's cheek, then lodged in the tree's trunk in front of us. My dragon roared at the sight of her blood staining her skin. But his roar was already growing weaker.

The dragon's bane was working.

A second and third arrow joined the first in the space of a few seconds. Elena spun to take stock, and found a fourth aimed straight for me. Without hesitation, Elena pushed me to the ground and put herself between the arrow and its intended target. I wanted to stop her, but my reflexes were nonexistent. All I could do was crumple to the ground and watch helplessly as the arrow flew straight toward her.

The impact threw her forward, and she caught herself

231

on her hands and knees. She screamed in pain, the sound tearing straight through me, and clutched at where the arrow was protruding from the side of her leg. If I could move, I would have ripped every one of them apart with my bare hands. I would have roasted them and left them for carrion.

"Elena!" I shouted. Or I thought I did.

She shook her head as though to clear it. Once her vision refocused, her eyes widened, and she scooted to my side, throwing her torso over mine to protect me from any stray arrows. My little mate. Protecting me. I would skin her hide for putting herself in danger if I ever survived this. The other girl, Leisha, had escaped, I think. I hoped she made it back to the castle without running into any humans.

"What are you still doing here?" I asked, though it cost me. My breathing was shallow, and my vision kept fading in and out.

"I'm not leaving you here." She studied the arrow and gritted her teeth. "Now do be quiet so I can save your hide before they strip it from your bones."

The arrow went clean through, so all she needed to do was break off the back and pull it the rest of the way. She ripped off a section of her cloak to use for bandages, wincing at its dirtied state, and threw it over her shoulder. With unsteady hands, she gripped the base of the arrow with her left hand to stabilize it and wrapped the other around the end.

"This may hurt," she told me.

Shouts and arrows came from behind—both at rapid speed—so she didn't have more time to waste. Instead, she took a few short breaths, then snapped the back of the arrow. I was so weak, I could only grunt in pain, even though it seared through my body like I imagined fire seared through my own victims. Without another moment's pause, she used her right hand and pulled from the front. I let out a high-pitched keen as the arrow tore through muscle and tissue.

Once the arrow was free, Elena took the strip from her cloak as quick as her numb fingers would allow and wrapped it twice around her leg to staunch the flow of blood, then used another strip to bind my shoulder. I watched her through a dense fog, only half aware of what she was doing. I wanted to tell her my wounds didn't hurt anymore, but didn't have the energy to speak.

She levered her body under my shoulder and used her good leg to get me on my feet, though it took some doing. Even as a human, I was still nearly twice her size.

"C'mon, they're getting closer," she urged.

"You smell so good," I said, nuzzling her hair as I leaned heavily against her side. "You always smell so damn good."

"Now is not the time, Rhys."

"I love it when you call me that." My voice was dreamy, dazed. This felt like a dream, like I was flying. I liked flying with her. "Do it again."

"I'll do it as many times as you like if you keep moving. If we can get over the hill up there, the main gates shouldn't be much farther. We can signal some of your men for cover until we get inside the castle walls."

"Scared—" I broke off to retch ineffectively into some bushes. "Scared the life out of me when Alaric came back and told me what was happening."

"It's all right, I'm here. I'm not going anywhere."

I didn't really give a damn if she was mad I had her followed. She could be mad all she liked. At least she'd be mad and safe.

"Promise me you'll keep yourself safe."

"No, I won't."

My voice grew stronger, and I used the remaining strength I had left to pull her behind a thick tree trunk. "Promise me, Elena."

"If you will stop carrying on so we can get to the castle in one piece, I'll promise you anything you bloody well want!"

"Tha's better," I slurred, slumping against her once more.

She turned us back toward the general castle, ignoring her own wounds. Keeping her eyes trained in front of us and her ears tuned to the humans behind us, she plowed her way through the drifts and trees until we reached the main road.

Orange orbs from the sconces on the castle walls led the way to the front entrance. The sound of the humans and their horses faded the closer we drew to the gate. A cry of alarm rent through the air when we were sighted and her knees threatened to buckle as Alaric rounded the corner, guards following behind.

He took my other side, his lips pressed into a thin line. Dazedly, I turned to him, clutching at his shoulder and nearly knocking Elena off her feet.

"You'll watch over her for me, won't you?" I stumbled over the uneven road. "The fae were after her."

"With my own life," Alaric assured me. "Bloody fae. I can't escape them."

"There will be none of that," Elena interjected. "Stop humoring him and help me get him inside."

"I'll thank you to cease giving me orders, my lady, considering that you're the reason he was shot in the first place."

We reached the front steps to the castle. Servants brought candles, bottles of tonic, and clean cloth. Alaric instructed them to be brought to my rooms. We stumbled through the labyrinthine corridors as I hovered between lucidity and delirium. By the time they laid me on my sprawling bed, I felt more like a corpse than a man.

Bruised and bloodied, Elena crawled onto the bed by my side, tucking her arm under my head and urging a maid to bring a mug of cool water. She held it to my lips and forced a few sips down my throat. I choked on it, already back into semi-unconsciousness.

"Why are you all standing here?" I heard Elena order. "Someone fetch the healer." When no one moved to do as she instructed, she said to Alaric. "Why aren't you doing anything to help him?"

I wanted to tell her she didn't need to worry. My life was for the short time I had her in it, but I didn't have the energy to form words.

Alaric's voice was mournful. "There's no helping him. They lace their arrows with dragon's bane for a reason."

"There has to be something you can do." Elena ran her fingers over my forehead. I loved having her hands on me. It made the gnawing inside my gut go away temporarily. "Anything," she begged

"Don't you think…" I said slowly, pausing to lick my chapped lips. "Don't you think if there was something we could do, we would have done it?"

"So you're just going to give up?"

Alaric hissed, and his boots ate the ground between them. "I'll not have you tossing about condemnations. The only thing we can do is wait. Sometimes the arrows aren't laced well enough, or sometimes they're removed before the blood can be properly infected. If we're lucky, he'll make it through the night."

"And if we're not lucky?" she asked.

"You best pray for a miracle."

WHISPERS FILLED THE BEDROOM. Servants milled about bringing finger foods and goblets of ale and lukewarm water. Stewards ushered in bowls of healing waters with fresh cloths. Alaric sat on a stool by the bed, his mouth a firm, disapproving line. I tossed back and forth on the bed, wondering if this was a fever dream or reality.

"What about the fae?" Elena asked. "They have magic. They must have a way to heal him. Their magick is very powerful."

"You haven't had enough of the fair folk tonight then, have you, my lady?"

"I haven't if they can help him." Elena was begging. I wanted to soothe her, but I couldn't find the energy to move. I settled for her touches, her kisses, and her closeness.

If Alaric noticed, he didn't comment, which showed great restraint on his part. "Well they can't, even if you could survive another encounter. They'd bleed you dry just for suggesting they help one of shifter blood. Especially Rhysander."

"And how would you know?" Elena hissed, clearly fed up with his unwillingness to help.

"They're my people. If I thought they would help I would move heaven and earth to save him."

Elena sighed. Then said, "Maybe my brother—"

"I'll not be trusting your brother with anything," Alaric spat with barely contained contempt.

"Do you have any ideas, then? Instead of dismissing all of mine, you might try to help."

"If I did it wouldn't be trusting the fae or your brother." Alaric laughed without humor. "You might as well be asking the bloodsuckers for help."

Elena paused, and I thought she might have given up on me. I wouldn't have minded. She'd thought of everything. She tried. That was all that mattered to me.

"What about vampires?" Alaric must have laughed when I drifted out, because Elena sat up and her voice was no nonsense. "No, I'm serious. I've heard rumors that they can heal the sick. How is this any different? Couldn't one suck the infected blood out?"

"If by heal the sick you mean turn them into the undead, then yes, by all bloody means why don't we invite one over for some tea and dragon blood?"

"Listen to me! You said if there wasn't enough blood infected with the poison that he may be able to recover.

What's stopping us from removing the blood altogether to prevent the infection? What have we got to lose, Alaric? It's our only chance to save him."

Alaric must have agreed because when I woke up, I knew Soren was there. His acidic voice filled my ears.

"If you think I'm going to drink from him, you're very well demented. The last thing I need is for the Dragon Lord to take offense and extend my punishment. I've already been all over the Northlands today doing his damned bidding."

"You'll do as I ask or I'll figure out a way to make your punishment permanent," Alaric warned.

Soren crossed the room with hesitant steps and towered over the side of the bed. "I can't promise that I'll be of any use to you. He could be too far gone for this to do any good."

"Then get on with it," Elena ordered. "If he dies because you couldn't stop yammering about, I'll kill you myself."

Alaric murmured appreciatively, Elena hovered over me protectively. Soren tilted my neck to the side and wet his lips and in the next moment his teeth lengthened into deadly points and he latched himself to my bared flesh.

I shuddered underneath Elena's hands and I hoped to Goddess she made the right decision. Soren motioned with a hand for the bowl and Elena gave it to him. He spat out blackened blood with a look of disgust, but returned again and again.

This went on until my feeble attempts at fighting Soren's embrace slackened and the grip I had on Elena's hand released. I didn't know if I was better or worse. I was spiraling into darkness.

Soren spat one final time into the bowl and wiped his mouth. "That's the last of it," he said. "You'll want to keep an eye on him when he wakes up. He's going to have a bitch of a headache and will probably feel sick to his stomach as well. Provided that the dragon's bane didn't reach his heart, he should make a full recovery. If he's lucky."

"Have you always been able to heal them like this?"

"From dragon's bane?" Soren said offhandedly, as he searched the room for something.

"Yes," Elena answered between gritted teeth.

He lifted the goblet of water next to the bed and peered inside it. He scowled and moved to the chest of drawers. "I've never done it before, so I can't tell you for sure."

"Then why would you…I mean what do you—"

Soren grinned. "What do I get in return?"

"Of course. We can take you anywhere you need to go. Alaric has transp—"

He waved a hand. "I'll not be needing a carriage, my lady."

Elena tensed beside me. "Then, what do you need?"

"What I was promised."

"And what was that?"

"In exchange for services rendered, the good man here bargained for blood. Yours," he elaborated.

I wanted to shout my disapproval, but I was fading fast.

The last thing I heard was, "Very well," Elena said. "Forgive me, but until I know for sure that my mate will survive, you won't be getting anything. Come morning, if he's still alive, you'll get what you were promised."

"I look forward to it."

ELENA

The sun rose and Rhys slept peacefully.

I didn't sleep a wink for fear I would wake and find him as lifeless and cold as the stone surrounding us. So when the first rays of morning light filtered through the bedroom drapes and illuminated his chest still rising and falling, a bone-deep weariness spread through me from top to toe.

My wounded thigh and mangled feet ached something fierce, but the pain was shadowed by the relief that he made it through the night. That we made it. I wasn't sure where we went from here, how we would deal with yet another threat, but I knew I couldn't lose him. I could face my own death, but I couldn't face his.

Even faced with the prospect of submitting to the vampire did little to dampen my spirits. When a knock came at the door and Soren peered in, a satisfied smile on his face, my relief turned to dread.

"Not one to waste any time, are you?" I commented. I wrapped my blanket around Rhys's waist and shifted down to the foot of the bed.

Soren's smile was feral, made even more so by his elongated canines. "I've thought of nothing else since I saw you. I do believe you will taste delicious. Certainly much better than your mate."

I refused to show weakness, even though I had to be trembling. "Glad to hear it. Do you mind if we get along with it? I'd like to get back to him as soon as possible."

"So eager," Soren drawled as he grew near.

"Eager to be done," I corrected.

Soren sat next to me on the foot of the bed. "Don't be so rash, love. You may find that you like it."

"Doubtful. And don't call me that." I resisted the urge to shrug away as he brushed hair away from my shoulder. He leaned forward, caressing my shoulder with his lips and I couldn't help but shudder.

In one swift movement, he jerked me sideways over his lap until he cradled me in his arms. Compared to Rhys, Soren was more lithe, but if the effortless way he bore my weight was any sign, he was not to be mistaken for weak.

His arms contracted, and he pulled me close to his chest. My hands rested on his shoulders and I squeezed my eyes shut. Being wrapped in another man's arms felt strange, forbidden, and unnatural. Soren was strange, forbidden and unnatural. When his cool lips touched my neck, I couldn't contain the shiver.

Then his mouth parted and his tongue lashed out to wet the skin. From what Alaric explained after he gave me to Soren as a reward for saving Rhys, it produced a numbing agent to make giving blood more enjoyable. In the moment before his fangs pierced my skin, I wondered how that could possibly be.

Then his teeth punctured my neck and my fingers gripped the material of his shirt to keep from falling into a boneless heap on the floor. Liquid pleasure raced across my nerve endings and I had to bite my tongue to swallow the moan that surface. Soren did little more than suckle at my neck, but I felt it everywhere.

I sensed myself becoming weak, though I couldn't discern if it was due to the blood loss or the state of euphoria. Someone spoke my name, but I didn't pay it any mind. I couldn't hear over the ringing in my ears anyway.

"*Elena,*" the voice said. I remembered enough for joy to spread throughout me, but I didn't understand why until it repeated the word.

"*Rhys?*" I wasn't sure if I said it aloud or thought it.

I blinked rapidly against the growing weariness. Soren still drew at my neck, but Rhys's voice pulled me away from the drunken stupor. I glanced back up at his body, finding him restless in sleep. A thin sheen of sweat covered his chest and his limbs twitched. His lips pulled down in a frown and his head lashed from side to side. Was he dreaming? I must have been imagining it. I'd give anything to hear his voice again. A part of me was certain I never would.

The tide of pleasure beckoned. My eyes drifted closed again when Rhys bolted straight up, his chest heaving and eyes bloodshot. A thrill shot through me and I clutched Soren, who hadn't seemed to notice.

"Stop."

Soren didn't heed his command, or maybe he didn't hear it. Rhys threw the sheets away and I struggled more insistently against the vampire's steel-like hold. The last thing Rhys needed was a fight with a vampire so soon after being injured.

"Get your hands off my mate," Rhys commanded. Even weak and near death, his dominance was absolute.

My hands repeatedly hitting his chest seemed to get Soren's attention, and he released, looking down at me quizzically. When Soren noticed my gaze elsewhere, he peered up and came face-to-face with Rhys.

"Ah, so it did work." Faced with an angry Rhys, Soren showed little to no change in his expression.

I wiggled out of his hold but my injured leg finally

gave out and I crumpled to the floor like a horse new to its limbs.

"Leave us," Rhys said, his eyes on me. The bedsheets pooled around his waist and even though he still looked white beneath his tan, he no longer seemed like he was seconds away from death.

Blood trickled down the side of my neck in a warm, wet slide and I couldn't bear to look at my mate as I remembered Soren's hands on my body. Warmth filled my cheeks, and I kept my eyes on my lacerated feet.

Soren backed away with a silky smile. "It's been a pleasure," he said before closing the door behind him.

The click of the lock echoed with finality. I kept my eyes on my feet, wishing very much that I'd been the one lost to sweet oblivion. It was my fault they hurt him. I shouldn't have been so careless. Despair mixed with regret. I hadn't been here a week, and I'd already caused so much trouble.

"I've never met anyone with such a disregard for their own safety." Rhys sighed, his forearms resting on his knees. "Protecting you has proven to be more work than twenty years of guarding the entirety of Acasia."

I was so sure!

Had I the energy I would have taken grave offense to that statement. "I'm too tired to argue with you," I said instead, eyelids drooping even as my words trailed off. "We can argue later."

He leaned down to offer a hand and I crawled toward him, gratefully. There may be a lot for us to talk about, a lot for us to work through, but I needed the reassurance of his body against mine, if only for a short while. He hefted me up and over his body on the other side of the bed. I crawled underneath the reassuring weight of the furs and toward the heat of his body. As we'd done a thousand other times it felt like, my head came to rest on his shoulder. It was difficult to resist the call to be close to my mate.

"I want to… thank you," he said carefully. "For saving my life."

I yawned, the reassuring beat of his heart steady in my ear. "I'm just glad you're okay."

He shifted beside me and a hand came to push the hair away from my face. I wished I had the energy to look up at him, to discern the meaning behind his tone, but my eyes simply wouldn't obey my commands. "When I've regained my strength, you'll get the punishment you deserve for putting yourself in danger in the first place."

I swallowed thickly, but held my tongue. Frankly, I felt like I deserved whatever punishment he levied, considering what I put him through, what I risked. Seeing him hovering so close to death wasn't a memory I was likely to forget, but was not punishment enough, I was certain.

"Did a healer look at your wounds?" Rhys asked, noting the blood staining my dress. I managed to pry my eyes open and glance down.

"No," I replied through another yawn, then snuggled closer. "We were more concerned about the dragon's bane than anything else. I'm sure I'll be fine."

Rhys cursed and shouted for the maids, who were no doubt hovering in the hallway awaiting his orders. "Bring the healer. Send for hot water and towels. Now," he barked when the maids stared at him wide-eyed, no doubt shocked by their master's sudden resurrection.

"Tell Alaric he's awake," I added more politely, remembering to add a 'please' at the end.

"Healer first," Rhys instructed, voice firm. "Her wounds need to be tended as soon as possible."

I inched closer to his warmth. "It's all right, Rhys. I barely feel it anymore." It was true. The anesthetic in Soren's bite washed away most of the pain. Or maybe it was the exhaustion. Either way, my injuries had ceased throbbing.

His arms tightened around me. "You're going to be the death of me," he muttered into my hair. The shifter inside of me reveled in his presence.

Then his words penetrated and I frowned. "That's not amusing."

"Quiet," he said.

My response was muffled against his chest as I

slipped back into unconsciousness. Through the haze of half-sleep, I heard the deep tones of Rhys's voice against my cheek. A flurry of activity commenced around me, but the only thing I cared about was the comforting circle of his arms.

"Come on now, Elena," he said. I batted him away with a hand and he sighed. "Wake up for me, baby." He lifted me up and my head lolled backward. I shied away from the bright candlelight, but Rhys shook me a little, forcing me to glare at him. "Come on now, you have to drink this."

I pushed the mug away. "I can't. I'm too tired."

"I know you are, love, but if you don't, that wound will fester and much as I enjoy your stubbornness, I enjoy your legs even more."

Rhys tucked a lock of hair behind my ear and I blinked up at him. He was leaning over me with one hand underneath my shoulders for support. He used his free hand to lift the mug to my lips. I managed to sip some of the bitter concoction and winced as the slimy brew slid down my throat.

"That's my girl." He sat the mug on the bedside table. "Now I'm going to get you out of those clothes so we can get you cleaned up."

Confused, I pulled away, glancing at the other people in the room. "Not now, Rhys. I'm tired."

He chuckled. "Much as that would stroke my ego,

we're only going to tend to your leg and feet." He leaned close and kissed my cheek. "*We'll save the rest for a time when we don't have a captive audience.*"

The strings of my corset loosened. Deft fingers worked the dress off my arms and over my hips. Left only in my chemise, I reclined back on the furs and tried to stay awake. Sharp pin pricks shot up and down my legs as Rhys and the healer began working on my feet.

"How did you know where to find me?" I asked, mostly to distract myself from the pain that had returned triple-fold.

"*Even if you weren't bound to me, I had Alaric keep close. I knew the moment you stepped of castle grounds. I could find you anywhere.*"

Not wanting his staff or Alaric to overhear the conversation, I thought my response instead. One day I'd be able to speak to him, like he did to me. "*I should have been more careful. I thought we would be safe since the orchards were near the castle. I won't make the same mistake again.*"

Rhys shook his head. "*It's not your fault. Someone wants you dead. I should have never let you leave the castle unprotected. These wounds are on me,*" he said with his eyes on the healer as they cleaned and dressed my legs and feet.

"*As yours are on me.*"

His hands tightened around me and it was a long

time before he spoke, so long I'd started drifting off. "*Sleep.*"

He leaned in to let his lips play lightly over mine. My hands lifted to hold on to his wrists and I made a panicked, delighted squeak of surprise.

The relief that flooded me was overwhelming. So much so, that I couldn't move as his mouth rubbed, as his teeth nibbled, and his tongue teased. I was frozen underneath him as pleasure and pain warred for dominance throughout my battered body. Noticing my response, Rhys tapered off and finished with his forehead pressed against mine.

"I understand, sweet. You must be dead tired. We'll talk about everything more later, when you're feeling better."

The healer finished patching up my feet and moved to the arrow wound in my thigh. I winced as he began to prod, but forced myself to focus on Rhys's face. "*Stay with me?*"

"*Always,*" he said.

We spent the following days in bed together, healing. If it weren't for the fear of losing him, I would have said they were some of the best days in my life. We talked about everything. I told him about my conversation with Leisha and how I had to dance for the fae. He told me when he realized something was wrong, and how he'd never flown so fast. The only thing we hadn't talked about...was his first mate. But I would not push him. Now more than ever, I believed he'd tell me about her when he was ready.

"What's this?" I asked, when Merry came in with a tray filled with food.

Rhys smiled devilishly. "It's for you."

He gestured for her to place the tray on a table by the bed and she left with a smile in my direction. There were tureens of steaming, buttery vegetables and platters of herbed meats. Also on the table was an arrangement of roses from the garden. Once he noted how much I enjoyed them, he made sure there were always fresh ones. Every time I scented a whiff of their fragrance, it brought a smile to my face.

"Thank you, this is wonderful. And beautiful. You didn't have to go to so much trouble."

"It's no trouble at all for you, my sweet. You need to build up your strength."

There were dishes I recognized, or that were at least similar to those we served in Aurelia such as the bitter-root, a potato-like root we roasted and served with herbs and pats of butter. I especially enjoyed the flank steak, though I didn't ask what animal it came from because I wasn't certain I wanted to know.

Even more than the food, I enjoyed spending time, actual time, with Rhys. Time where we didn't have to travel—didn't have to rush to be somewhere. Time where it was just the two of us—with no interruptions. I hated it had to come under these circumstances, but I was going to enjoy it while it lasted.

"What's that smile for?" Rhys asked, once the dessert dishes were cleared away and steaming mugs of the Northlands coffee were served.

"This has been the best day," I said. "I don't think it can get any better."

"I'll take that as a challenge."

I giggled, perhaps from the wine, perhaps because being bound to Rhys was turning out to be everything I'd ever dreamed up, but never thought I could have. "What are we going to do now? I couldn't possibly eat anything else."

Rhys took my hand and drew me close. "Then you'll have to leave the eating to me."

"Now, Princess, didn't I tell you to lie still?"

I nearly screamed in frustration. In the two hours since Rhys had cleared away the food, he'd stripped me of my clothes and brought me to the edge of climax so many times I'd lost count.

"I can't," I managed to say through heaving breaths. "Rhys, please. I can't take it anymore."

"You can. You can take whatever I'll give you." The sting of his teeth on my inner thigh caused me to gasp. "Won't you?"

I couldn't answer. There weren't any words left inside of me that didn't include more, please, harder, or his name. The only thing I wanted was him, but it was the one thing he wouldn't let me have. It was like he knew how to give me just enough to make me want more, beg for more, but deny me just when I was nearly satiated. It was maddening. Fever stole over me, smoldering and suffocating. It blotted out everything but the shadow of him crouched, waiting between my spread legs.

The mark on my neck pulsed in time with the furious tattoo of my heart. It, too, wanted. Needed. The thread connecting us both had never been clearer. He alternately tortured and tempted me, and each time, I got flashes from him. Of how I looked from his point of view, spread out much like the dinner we'd feasted on. I'd heard him say without words how much he wanted to feast on *me*.

The longer he'd drawn out the seduction, the more the walls between us dropped, the clearer the connection between us had gotten. It thrummed like a constant hum inside me, wanting, needing me to make the connection complete. I didn't know how to do whatever it wanted me to do. Rhys seemed to be working toward something with ruthless intent, but I was mindless to anything but when he would touch me again.

"Won't you?" he repeated.

My head thrashed back and forth against the pillow as his mouth hovered over me, his breath lightly playing over the overstimulated intimate flesh. When his mouth latched onto me, and his tongue unleashed a relentless assault, I cried out and my feet dug into the quilted patchwork of muscles on his back, so I could lift my hips to meet what felt like my own damnation.

He paused and when he spoke his lips brushed over

me with each word. "Can you take it? Do you want me to stop?"

The thought was so abhorrent, I reached down with a guttural cry that sounded nothing like me and pressed his mouth back to me, using my grip on his hair to keep him in place.

But of course that didn't stop him. He merely spoke directly to my mind. *"I can keep this up all night, pet. I can bring you to the brink of pleasure and deny you. Again and again until you give me what I want."*

"What do you want?" I asked, my voice breaking with force of desperation.

"I want you to tell me you'll take it. Take it all. You'll have me, in every way, just as much as I'll have you. I want you to be my mate in all things as long as you'll have me. Claim me as I have you."

I couldn't have stopped the wave of pleasure if I'd tried. I crested, seized underneath him, his fingers digging into my hips, my feet scrabbling on the bed for purchase as it overtook me. It was like he called it forth by words alone, like he understood and played my body better than I could. But the orgasm didn't satisfy me. If anything, it only intensified the hunger.

He crawled up my limp and throbbing body, a god in his own right, this man who'd pledged himself to me, came to my aid. This man who wanted to be mine as more than just in name only. Sweat sheeted his body, glinting in the moonlight shining through the bare windows that peered out into the open night. Candlelight flickered in his brilliant gold eyes as he came to rest on top of me, the brunt of his weight on his forearms.

"I need you, Elena."

I could hear the truth in his words, see it through our bond. The pleasure I took from them was almost as great as the pleasure he'd given my body. He needed and wanted *me*. Not just because I was a princess, not because I could give him something in return. He wanted me forever, without restraint.

For that reason, I shifted underneath him and reached for the heavy length of his erection and guided it to where I waited, empty and aching. He rolled his hips in one graceful movement and the feel of him gliding inside me stole my breath. There was something so explicit about the first breach, something so carnal and primitive. If I had a shifter form, I knew it would be clawing at me to shift, to mark him in some way that he would have visible signs of our union.

Rhys's dragon had come out to play. There were light red score marks over the pearly white of my flesh from when his fingers had lengthened into claws. He used them over the tips of my breasts, down the sensitive skin of my sides and on the inside of my thighs. Not enough to draw blood, but enough that it came rushing to the surface to sensitize me to every touch in those areas.

I wanted things I'd never wanted before. To draw blood, to give into an animalistic state I hadn't even been aware existed.

I wanted to lose control.

I wanted him to lose control.

It was both terrifying and exhilarating.

Alluring and horrifying.

I didn't even have a choice in the end. My body made the choice before my mind could catch up. I screamed in pain as a great heat seared my neck. At first I didn't understand what was happening, but then I heard Rhys's voice inside my head, talking me through it, his tone soothing and I followed it out of the pain until I resurfaced.

His face was the first thing I saw.

He brushed the damp hair out of my face. "Shh, love, everything is fine."

For a moment, I fought him, reacting on instinct, then I relaxed underneath him. His stroking hands, his calm voice allowed my heartbeat to slow and my muscles to unclench.

"What in Goddess' name was that?" I gasped, when I calmed down enough to speak.

Rhys didn't have any words for my question. I drew my hands up to his face and lifted him from where he'd been buried in my neck. "Rhys? Are you okay? Did it hurt you, too?"

He trembled against me and I sucked in a breath when I realized he was still hard, possibly even more than he'd ever been any time we'd made love.

"What happened?" I asked again.

He struggled for breath. Instead of answering, he said, "Let me show you."

My brows furrowed, and I opened my mouth to ask him what he meant when a vision blotted out the room. It was me, I realized after a stunned moment. Me, as Rhys saw me. I burned with embarrassment when I saw my face. Hair was plastered to my skin, my cheeks were ruddy with a blush, and I still hadn't caught my breath completely. I was about to make a comment about my appearance when I caught the sight of the mark I'd received the night of the binding ceremony.

"Holy stars," I breathed.

The mark had been snow white, even against my creamy skin. I'd grown used to seeing it in the mirror and hadn't given it much thought since arriving at the castle. Now, it was burned into my throat with a black ink, a stark contrast to my pale skin.

"No," I said without thinking. "No, we can't. This can't be."

I struggled underneath him, wriggling and writhing, but only managing to make us both breathless as he was still poised over me and still very much aroused and inside of me.

"Let me go," I said. A wildness was overtaking me. My only thought was that I needed to get away. Needed to flee as far and as fast as I could.

He bared his teeth, nearly snarling with intensity. "If you think I'm ever going to let you go, you are sorely mistaken."

He began to move then, and it was like nothing I'd ever felt before. Pleasure so intense seared me from all directions. From the physical stimulation, from the mental link he'd opened somehow between us, and through the bond itself. It was an assault of the senses for which there was no defense.

"Please," I begged. "I can't. You have to let me go."

"You're not going anywhere."

He thrust with an aching tenderness I didn't even know he was capable of, like I was made of glass, fragile and delicate. His mouth coasted over my face, his lips and tongue caressing and tasting me as though he couldn't get enough. He worked his arms underneath my shoulders, his hands turning palm up so he could use them as a counterpoint against his thrusts, which were still frustratingly slow.

"Rhys, you don't want this. You don't want me like this. Anything could happen! I could die. You could be killed. You don't understand," I said thoughtlessly.

His face didn't darken, but shadows appeared in his eyes, like the ghosts of those things he had lost. "I do understand. Trust me, Elena, I understand more than you can imagine."

"Then, *why?*" I cried. "Why would you risk losing everything again?"

"Because the true loss wouldn't be losing you. It would be never having tried to keep you."

I ached with such beauty that I wanted to cry. "I don't know if I'm strong enough," I confessed.

"I've never known anyone with more strength," he said solemnly. "Fall with me."

Before my eyes, I watched as he arched his own neck, baring to me as his own mark flashed in the moonlight, then solidified as mine had into a permanent brand. A claiming mark. The bond between us was complete. Absolute. His rhythm faltered, but the same couldn't be said for the bond between us. I grasped his shoulders, as it seemed to explode, blotting out the light, the room, the world.

RHYSANDER

She was mine. Irrevocably.

We may go down in flames, but for now, we belonged to each other. The marks on our throats were visible to other shifters for a reason. In the days of old, the claiming marks were a show of strength between bonds, to let other clans know the connection between mates was strong and therefore the clan was strong. It was also rare. And powerful, I hoped.

Powerful enough to break a curse.

"I have a surprise for you," I told her the next morning.

"What surprise?" she asked. "Can't we stay in bed again?"

"I'd love nothing more than to stay in bed with you for the next century, but there is something I want to show you. I wouldn't ask if it wasn't important. You should probably get dressed," I added reluctantly.

"I understand." She walked naked to her closet, my eyes on her swaying hips the entire way there. "Should I cover up the mark? It'll be obvious what happened."

I cleared my throat after a lengthy pause then cleared it again. "There hasn't been a completed bond in my clan for years. Not since before the curse. They will no doubt be ogling. Let them. I want everyone to know you're mine."

She returned, dressed in one of the new gowns I'd purchased for her, a light blue shimmery fabric that floated around her ankles like delicate snowflakes. I went to her, drinking her in with my shirt still untucked from my pants and undone at the throat. Even half-dressed she was utterly delicious.

Her throat bobbed as she swallowed. I didn't have to read her mind to know some part of her enjoyed how possessive I could be. I laid a hand over the mark on her throat. My eyes drifted closed and a sound of pleasure escaped my lips.

"I'm glad it was you," I said, before pressing a kiss to her surprised mouth.

"*Me, too,*" she answered in my head.

"Come on," I said after fastening her dress. A combination of nerves and dread writhed in my stomach. She followed, content to let me lead and explain what we were doing in my own time. I was grateful. It would take the brief walk to our destination for me to work up the courage anyway. She was quiet, letting me lead her through the castle to the entrance for the crypts.

"Where are you taking me?" she asked, as I tugged her along a dark, cavernous tunnel. Her injuries were as healed as they were going to get and I no longer required a nap every afternoon to be at full strength. It was the second time she had saved my life, nearly sacrificing her own to do it. There wouldn't be a better opportunity to lay it all bare for her than this one.

"If I told you, that would ruin the surprise." I led her around a corner, her hand in mine. I could have let her read my thoughts now that the connection between us was completely open, but I wanted to show her, to explain to her. I wanted to give her this truth myself now that there were no walls between us.

"Don't you think we've had enough surprises?" she asked wryly.

"A good surprise," I said, and I hoped it would be true.

"These are the crypts, aren't they? I thought I wasn't supposed to go down here. Alaric told me I shouldn't."

"I told him to tell you that. I didn't want you to see it without me. I wasn't ready—I didn't know how to tell you what I needed to until now."

She was quiet again as we moved deeper into the

mountains. It felt right to have her here. I never thought I'd be able to share anything so personal with anyone, but she was my mate and she belonged here. She deserved to know all of my secrets.

The closer we got to our destination, the colder it became. The light was dim, tinged with a blue-green hue. Magick pulsed as though it was a living thing, making the hair on my arms stand up.

The hallway narrowed and soon we were squeezing through a space that only left a few inches for us to maneuver. When it opened up again, Elena looked up from where she was navigating through the rock and gasped, but the sound of surprise was drowned out by the constant pattering of water from the dark heights of the endless room. It seemed to suck up most of the sound, but not the buzzing hum that came from everywhere and nowhere all at once.

There were eggs, as far as the eye could see. Hundreds of them. Thousands. Maybe even tens of thousands. They were displayed on pedestals and glowed—the source of the blue-green light that illuminated the room. Inside the eggs, shadow forms writhed and danced. Her hand went to her mouth, and tears sprung to her eyes. This part I didn't have to explain. These were thousands of potential lives that may never be born, cursed to a sort of half-life locked inside the shells, waiting. The part of me that drove the mating lust ached fiercely at the sight, and I thought of the hatchlings we might not ever have.

"When I told you I wanted you to give me an heir, I hadn't been lying. All I've ever wanted was to break the curse that kept my people from their birthright. I hope when the time is right, we can make one of these lives together." She was too shocked to speak, so I kept going. "But before that happens, I want to tell you about Valeria. Then, if you want to leave and never come back, I won't stop you."

"I'm listening," she said.

I pushed a hand through my hair, then gestured for her to sit with me on the steps. Her beautiful face was awash in the blue-green glow, her expression patient and open. I didn't deserve her. Not one bit.

"My first mate wasn't a nice woman. She came from a long line of distinguished clansmen. Our binding had been arranged since we were hatchlings. I didn't have an opinion one way or another. Having a mate was my duty. It wasn't until after we were bound that I realized what she was."

Elena's hand convulsed over mine. "What do you mean?" She licked her lips as though her mouth had gone dry with fear. Or maybe that was just mine.

"Valeria was...cruel," seemed to be the best way to explain it.

"She was cruel?" Elena repeated. "To you?"

I looked away. "Sometimes." I wanted to tell her, wanted to lay my heart bare, but the words were so hard to get out. I didn't want her to think less of me.

"She hurt you?" Elena prodded gently.

"She tried. I was much bigger, much stronger. I could have stopped her, but she always made me feel like I deserved it."

"Oh, Rhys. Of course you didn't."

"She was very convincing, very clever. And I would never raise a hand to a woman, despite my reputation. So I took it, for years, because I thought it was my duty to be her mate, produce sons."

Her breath caught as she remembered how this particular story ended, but she didn't interrupt.

"One day, she was trying to provoke an emotion out of me, any emotion. Normally, I'd give in and give her the argument she was looking for, but I was tired of fighting her. So tired. All I wanted was for her to go away and I think she knew it." Elena wrapped her arms around me. I felt the shudder of her breath against my side. I pushed on. "I tried to leave her screaming behind me and she followed me to the aviary platform. I told her I was done. That we'd have the bond annulled. I couldn't do it anymore."

"I didn't even know that was possible."

"Neither did I until I'd been pushed too far, for too long."

"What did she say to that?"

"She told me if I went through with it, she'd kill herself and that I'd be sorry."

Elena wrapped her arms around me. She was shaking. So was I.

"I told her I was going to go through with the annulment. I didn't think she'd also go through with it. What I didn't know was she'd gone to a caster for a curse." At this Elena stiffened. "She'd had a powerful caster put a curse on our clan. No dragon would ever fly the skies or have another hatchling until I could convince another Immortal to learn to love a beast like me. I think the curse was more powerful than either she or the caster intended. As time went on, it grew stronger until I was the only dragon left."

She put her hands on either side of my face. "None of this was your fault. No one deserves to be treated like that. No one. And I will never hurt you like she did, Rhysander Blaque. I promise you as long as I live, you'll never have to fear me."

I kissed her, pulled her close, and put everything I was feeling into it. "I know that, little mate. I hope you'll forgive me."

"For what?" she asked.

"For treating you like a means to an end. If I could go back, I'd do it differently. If I never break the curse, but get to have you in my life, then being your mate would be more than worth it."

After my confession, Elena held me for a while, then pulled back and studied my expression, letting her mind inch along our connection to test the waters of my mood. She hadn't been able to tell I was hiding things from her before, but maybe she hadn't been paying close enough attention. The surge of our bond was so intense, she jerked backward the second she came in contact with my mind.

I watched as tears streamed from her eyes. Her thoughts, her feelings, became my own. For the first time since we'd met, since we realized we were mates, we could...*feel* each other. All of each other. Without restraint or restrictions, lies or boundaries. One of us, I wasn't sure who, reached out, gripped each other's hands and pulled closer. I held her too tight, but I only paid half-attention, too intrigued by the siren call of her soul across our connection.

What would it be like to know every little thing about him? she thought.

The prospect—and its implications for her—were staggering.

She struggled to focus on my face as I shared memories about her from my point of view. The day we met in her father's room. Embracing me for the first time by the creek. Our binding ceremony and the night after. The dinner. Seeing her face when I realized I was infected with dragon's bane. Her saving me. Claiming her.

"It's all right," I said, and then reached out through our connection to her. When her knees buckled, I gripped her arms and held her steady. All the while I murmured softly in her ear, "Don't be afraid. I'm here. I'm not going anywhere. Yes, sweet, hold onto me. I won't let you go."

An indeterminate amount of time passed before she was able to control the door she'd opened between us. When she regained the ability to stand, she did so on trembling legs. The mating bond between us before had been staggering. She'd never felt so happy or content. I didn't think being bound to her could get any better.

Until now.

"I didn't want to see what we could be at first," I said, my voice a rumble in the darkened caves. The steady *drip, drip* of water in the distance made it seem like we were alone for miles. "I was afraid to lose you. To fail you like I'd failed Valeria. I was so afraid to lose you that I pushed you away. It took nearly losing you to realize we are worth that risk."

She opened her mouth to speak, but I kissed away her protests.

"No matter what happens to the clan, or with the humans, I'm glad I have you and I'm *never* going to let you go again."

"I believe you," she said. When we were both steady again, I helped her to her feet. "How far do these go?" she asked, gesturing to the eggs.

"I like to use these caves to think. I guess I've walked miles of them and have never seen an end. When my father was alive, he used to say they went on forever."

"Forever?"

"Mmhmm. The mountain was blessed by magic. These crypts could come out on the other side of the world, for all we know. We used to explore them a lot— when there were more of us."

"I've never seen our own unborn in the palace. They were kept under strict guard. For exactly this reason, I suppose."

I led her through dozens of rows until we came to several on a ledge near a far wall. We stopped, and I pivoted to her.

She stared at them. "These are yours." It wasn't a question.

"Ours," I said, and my voice was as hoarse as hers. "These would be ours."

She reached out to them automatically, a yearning passed through the connection, and it took me a few seconds to put a name to it. She wanted these babies. Our babies. She wanted them with a fierceness that obliterated every doubt and worry I could imagine. The strength of her longing made her reach out for me. I met her hand without a word.

"Can I?" she asked, but I was already reaching to lift one glowing orb from its stand.

As I brought it closer, the shadowy, ethereal movements became more visible. Or at least the barest shifting of light. We were holding a little soul—our future child—in our hands. I shifted closer and my chest pressed against Elena's back. In that moment with her in my arms holding our future, I felt her understanding. She knew why I was willing to risk everything to save these lives. She flung out her thoughts, searching for me, and I caught her without hesitation.

When the time was right, if we ever broke the curse, one of these souls would choose us to bring them into this world. It was an honor above all others. One I hoped we'd get to experience together.

"*I want this with you,*" she said.

I released a long, slow breath and wrapped my hands around her waist and held her so close there wasn't a breath between us.

"*You won't regret it.*"

We stood there for a long time. I wasn't sure how long because there was no light save for the eggs. Tears slicked down her cheeks, and I held her as long as she liked.

I tucked my face into her neck as she cradled the egg

in her hands. "I love you, Elena," I said aloud, and for a second the words echoed around us without response.

She turned to me, slowly. "What did you say?" she asked.

A little smile tugged at my lips and I moved closer, the heat around us snapping and crackling with dangerous intent. Emotions swirled between us, held aloft by a turbulent storm, whipped into a frenzy by hope and elation.

As though she were the most delicate thing I'd ever beheld, I caressed her face with the back of my fingers, then kissed her eyelids, then her nose, and finally her mouth.

"I love you," I said.

She pulled me close, needing the three-fold connection, craving her touch. The moment my lips touched hers, the air around us became charged with electric heat. I swear I could hear it sizzle as her tongue met my own and my hands touched everywhere I could reach.

Finally, our bond said.

The connection between us, without barriers, was indescribable. Joyous, terrifying, heart-wrenching. A maelstrom. It was as though we were forged by the same blacksmith, from the same ore. A lock and its matching key. Wrought from unbreakable metals and tested by the brightest flame.

"Take me to bed," she moaned against my lips. "I need you."

"We may not make it to the bed," I warned as I cursed.

Elena replaced the egg with care, and then we began to stumble through the pedestals.

We were halfway across the never-ending room, when I surfaced enough to realize the eggs didn't look the same. Elena must have noticed it too because she tugged at my hand to slow me down.

"Look," she whispered, afraid to speak too loudly and stop the sight before me.

"What's wrong?" I asked, then I followed her gaze.

What I saw made my hand tighten painfully around hers, but she didn't seem to notice.

All I could focus on were the eggs. Which were shining even more brightly. Their incandescence was almost hard to behold, and we had to squint in order to see.

"What…what does this mean?"

I was at a loss for words. "We must find Alaric."

We were nearing the room's exit, the eggs still glowing madly, when we heard a great crash and the caves shuddered under the impact, dust showering down and rocks shaking loose and shattering in the halls.

I met her gaze and I didn't need to say a word. She already knew what I was thinking.

We were under attack.

24

ELENA

There was a moment's pause before Rhys shifted, his claws and teeth elongating and the scales on his skin hardening and losing their translucence.

"Stay behind me," he ordered.

I gave one last look to the cave where our future lay and reassured myself that the magic protecting the eggs would hold. It would have to. We would have to.

We didn't make it far before Rhys paused, holding a hand to my stomach to stop me in the middle of the hall.

"*Someone's coming,*" he said.

"*Humans?*" I asked and hoped my fear wouldn't translate through our bond.

If it were humans armed with dragon's bane again, Rhys was as good as dead. Soren was long gone, and it wasn't like we could round up another vampire on a whim.

"*I'm not sure*," Rhys said. "*Whatever we do, we can't let them get to the eggs or the clan.*"

"*I'm ready*," I said. "*We won't.*"

We crept through the caves as quietly as we could, but it didn't matter. The noise coming from the exit was deafening and covered any sounds we made. Screams and shouts echoed off the stone walls. The sound of pinging arrows and cannon fire made it seem as though shots were coming in all directions. Each time I heard the loud rapport from a cannon followed by the *thunk* and *boom* I ducked instinctually. Rhys took me by the shoulder, hauled me to my feet and kept moving.

It was the thought of all those little lives behind me that kept me moving forward toward danger instead of running in the opposite direction like I wanted to do. Finally, we made it to the exit, but I dreaded seeing what was on the other side. With a signal to me to keep back, Rhys crept forward and peered around the door's edge.

I waited impatiently, my hands clapped over my mouth, body wracked with shivers as cannons blasted relentlessly. I wanted to cover my ears as well, but I didn't want to miss it if Rhys gave me any instructions. As I waited, my muscles so tense they ached, I remembered Rhys telling me about the entire town they had massacred. In their weakened state the Dragon-Clan was an easy target for those armed with dragon's bane. To what end and for what reasons, I couldn't say. But we would find them. And we would stop them, whatever the cost.

Rhys came to my side, and all I wanted to do was take him in my arms, but I forced myself to recall the steadiness I'd learned as a healer. I could help them. I had to.

"Stay behind me at all times," he said in a low voice. "We'll lead them away from the caves and to the outside, if we can. Away from the castle and the village to decrease fatalities. I need for you to find Alaric and tell him to have the guards circle around. We'll get them in a bunch and I'll turn the lot of them to ash once and for all."

"I can do that," I said with a certainty that surprised me. Since when had I become the sort of person to rush into danger instead of run from it?

Rhys gathered me close, his expression fierce, as he pressed a hard, urgent kiss on my lips. "I love you," he said.

Before I had a chance to respond, he was rushing into the melee with a battle cry that drew all attention to him. He shifted in an explosion and burst into the sky.

This was my chance. I didn't have a moment to think about how scared I was, how I was the wrong person for the job, a coward who'd run from her own family, her own kingdom. Instead, I threw myself into the fight. All eyes were on Rhys as he battled a path through the army of humans.

I hadn't gotten a good look at them the day they nearly killed Rhys, but they were unmistakable. Shrouded in dark-colored swaths of fabric, they were dirty, unkempt, and reeked of sour skin. I hoped they would be easy to track based on smell alone.

The thick of the fighting was centered at the front of the castle. Those I recognized from the Dragon-Clan emblem they wore on their chests were knotted with the foul-smelling humans. But it was the bloodied maids uniform that gave me pause. Near the rose garden, a tell-tale skirt with a white apron peeked out from around the corner. At first I thought it was just a rose, until I drew closer and recognized the skirt.

It was just like the one Leisha and Merry wore.

My heart froze in my chest and I inched around the grand columns that decorated the main hall until I got close enough to the garden for a clear view. I shouldn't have. The sight of the mangled body brought bile rushing to my lips, but I managed to keep it down. Leisha's face was imprinted on the back of my eyelids as I tore my eyes away from the sight of her battered face.

Find Alaric, came Rhys' voice from my memory. I latched onto it and used it like a lodestone to distract me from the horror I'd just seen. *Find Alaric.*

I spotted his golden hair battling two humans on the

grand staircase and slinked my way around two columns to get a closer look. He moved with an inhuman grace that the two clumsy humans could barely match. Within seconds, he'd skewered one, then used his boot to remove the sword from his chest. It released with a distinct sucking sound. Then, he pivoted to the other, who'd watched the entire scene with his mouth bared in a grimace revealing blackened teeth. Alaric took advantage of the human's surprise and slashed a gaping smile into his throat. By the time I regained my wits, he was bounding down the stairs.

Before he could escape, I yelled as loud as I dared, "Alaric!" and thanked the stars for his enhanced hearing because fear had choked my scream to a croak. He turned at his name and searched the shadows until he landed on me. His eyes widened in surprise and he changed directions.

"Where is he?" he asked without preamble.

Somewhat out of breath, I said, "He's fighting them off, he wanted me to find you."

Before I could finish explaining the plan, he'd already made off toward the cluster of humans and guards. I had to race to catch up to him and even then he tried to shake me off and swat me away like an annoying fly.

"Alaric, stop! Rhys said we need to gather the guards and herd the humans outside. He'll attack them from the skies and pick them off." But Alaric wasn't listening. He was too busy studying the fight.

He shook me off and spun around. "Let's go."

Relief speared through me. All it would take was one more arrow dipped in dragon's bane for me to lose my whole world. The fear I already had propelled me forward. I took out the dagger I'd stored at Rhys' insistence and used it to take down two humans who crossed my path, as we traversed the entry hall and fought our way back to Rhys's side.

By the time we made it, Rhys and his guards had cornered most of the humans by the front doors. What they didn't have in power, they made up for in numbers, swarming the front steps like ants. Alaric and some others herded the few stragglers back to the group. We were winning, I realized. We would win.

Rhys was in a half-shift, using his armored scales to block the slashing knives and knock away arrows with inhuman reflexes. He used the wicked points of his claws to slash and maim any human stupid enough to get too close. We fought by his side, defending his back as the humans tried to rush his vulnerable spots. As he'd been instructed, Alaric directed the castle guards to block the humans in and start pressing them toward the exit.

Then, just as we nearly had them right where we wanted them, a shout came from the back of the knot of humans. They'd spotted something in the distance.

Something that made them crow and cheer. One by one, they ran—away from us and toward the newcomers.

The castle guards looked at each other, then at Rhys, in confusion. Even Alaric's face was ravaged with concern. The fact that the humans were cheering outside of the castle made ice ball up in my stomach. I'd never hated the mortals before that moment. I'd never wanted to kill when all I'd ever done was heal, but I felt rage licking at my insides.

Rhys came to my side and the guards followed closely behind. Alaric kept his place by Rhys's other side and we all began to move toward the sound of cheers. Whatever it was—it couldn't be good.

At first the brilliant white from the moon was blinding and I winced, holding a hand up. Then, as my eyes adjusted to the light, I realized what—or rather who —was waiting just outside the castle.

I would recognize the colors they flew anywhere. But it wasn't the flags they flew that made the bottom drop out of my stomach. It was the man posed on the first horse of the line.

A man who shared my features.

Who raised me.

The man I'd always trusted.

My *brother*.

I took a few stuttering steps forward before Rhys saw

what I was doing and jerked me back, his claws digging into my stomach in his haste.

I fought him, not completely understanding what was going on.

"*Calm*," he said. "*Don't do anything rash.*"

"What are you doing here?" I asked Gideon. My brain couldn't comprehend it. Had he come to save me from Rhys? Had he come because father had died? Something about that niggled at my brain, but I couldn't place it.

All I knew without a doubt was that he shouldn't be here. He should be in Aurelia, with our people. A part of me knew that he wouldn't leave the capital unless there was a good reason. The only reason he'd come here, with a contingent of soldiers, was for war, but that didn't make sense in my brain.

Gideon wouldn't go to war with the man he demanded I mate. He couldn't.

But when he spoke, it wasn't to me.

"Stand down," Gideon said to Rhys in that commanding way of his. "Stand down and no one has to get hurt."

The humans scowled and yelled, but Gideon quieted them with a murderous look.

"Careful, Darkmoore," Rhys said, his voice as threatening as a thunderclap. "We're not in the capital anymore. You have no power here."

"Really?" Gideon said, though he didn't seem worried by Rhys's thinly veiled warning.

At a jerk of his head, more humans exploded from the castle. Where in Slaine had they come from? For the first time panic threatened to overwhelm me, and the small amount of bravado I'd conjured shrank inside me. The humans surround us with spear-tipped lances held at the throat of every Dragon-Clan guard.

The threat against the people who would willingly lay their lives down for me allowed me to find my voice. "Gideon, what are you doing here? Tell them to back off."

But he didn't answer me. Instead, he jerked his head again, and two humans with sickeningly gleeful smiles that made my stomach turn moved toward me, one of them jangling a chain with each step. Rhys made to stop them, but the human with the spear pointed at his neck pressed dangerously close.

"No!" I screamed and threw myself in between my husband and certain death. "No," I repeated through gritted teeth. "I'll do whatever you want. Just don't hurt him."

Gideon finally looked at me. "You'll do whatever I want, regardless, *Sister*."

At his nod, the two humans forced me to my knees in front of Rhys, who stood with barely restrained fury. His scales flashed, his eyes shifted from my beloved blue to blinding with startling swiftness, and all the while smoke unfurled from his nose. Each time he swallowed, his throat bobbed against the tip of the spear and I died a little inside.

All I could think was that I never got the chance to tell him I loved him back.

"Why are you doing this?" I asked, as the two humans bound my arms to my ankles with the chains. Snow soaked the thin material of my dress, but I ignored the cold. Shock numbed everything but the fear. "This is the legacy you honor Father with?"

If he was even still alive.

"Fuck his legacy," Gideon spat, as he dismounted his horse and stalked to me. "He made our clan weak, pining after mother. Now he'll suffer just as much as you will for underestimating me all these years." His eyes glinted in the moonlight like the steel blade he brought against my throat.

"But you sent me to the temple. You wanted me to mate Rhys—"

"He was never supposed to save you. You were supposed to die the day your wine was poisoned before you ever left the Goddess-forsaken castle! Then the humans would have attacked the castle when it was most vulnerable and I would have been rid of you both and Seleste in one go! Instead, I had to kill her with my own hands, and now I've come to take care of you myself.

When I'm done, I'll be King and no one will ever forget my name again."

There was a viciousness in his eyes that I'd never seen. A ruthlessness. I couldn't reconcile the monster in front of me with the man who'd been there for me my whole life.

The tears that had been such a constant companion over the last few years were noticeably absent. As I stared up into my brother's face, my face was dry. He wouldn't get the satisfaction of seeing me squirm.

"Now you know what it's like to lose everything," Gideon said to Rhys, whose eyes had gone completely black. Not even the whites were visible. "I was going to get the throne until you came along and made the deal with father. If it hadn't been for you, I would have been King twenty years ago."

Any hope I had that Gideon was pretending for the humans' sake was extinguished when he allowed the human closest to him to take the knife at my throat. The human eyed Rhys with barely contained glee.

"I've spent decades waiting for this moment," Gideon taunted Rhys. "You and the other shifters have terrorized the mortals for too long."

"Like you care what happens to them," Rhys growled. "They're a means to an end for you."

The human with the knife at my throat laughed. "You know, after you killed most of my clan, I thought all I wanted was to see your head on a pike, but I think I'm feeling generous." He circled me with the knife still at my throat. "Or maybe I'm enjoying the thought of you in pain and at my mercy, wondering, worrying, for the rest of your life what horrors I'm subjecting your sweet little mate to."

"We don't have all day," Gideon said. "I want to get back to the castle and out of the cold. Take care of this now, or I'll do it myself."

"Gideon, how could you?" I whispered.

"How could I?" he said, striding to where I knelt. "Very easily. You spent your childhood traipsing around the castle like you didn't have a care in the world," he sneered. "You were to be Queen, even though you couldn't even shift. You're even more pathetic than I thought."

He moved away, then, his face growing slack from boredom. I heard his footsteps, but I couldn't track him. I wanted to shout, to rail at him, but one of the humans slammed the hilt of knife against my temple. Rhys howled in protest, and jerked away from the guards who'd had his arms. Three others piled on him, each battering him with their fists and heavy boots. He fought back valiantly, but took a hit to the head that had him going ever so still.

I tried to shout, but my mouth had filled with blood from the wound on my head where they'd hit me, which made breathing, let alone talking unbearable. Around me, the humans had battered the guards and Alaric was fighting four at once—and losing.

Rhys still hadn't woken.

A part of me wasn't sure if he ever would, which made the fact that my lungs were screaming from a shot to the ribs a little easier to bear. Somehow I knew the pain couldn't last forever. It couldn't last forever and once it was over, I'd be with Rhys again. There was some comfort to be found in that.

Spots dotted my vision, but I could still see where Rhys lay beside me. It took effort, strength that I didn't even know I had, but I jerked my body sideways so I could reach him. It took all the rest of my energy, but I managed to get close enough to rest my head on his brow. Blood still poured freely from the wound on his cheek, but it didn't matter.

I could sense him through the connection of our bond, but it was tenuous. I wasn't sure if that was because I could feel myself fading fast or because he was unconscious. As the black spots began to cloud my vision and blot out the sight of his face, I decided I didn't have the energy to figure it out. With the last of my strength, I screamed out for him with all that I had left, and I could only hope it reached him.

I wanted him to know I loved him, too.

RHYSANDER

When I woke, everything hurt. But not as much as the sight of my mate, bloodied and broken, in front of me. Her beautiful dark curls were sticky and matted with blood and mud and snow. Her face was covered with it and the growing shadows of bruises. The sight of her wounds filled me with immeasurable anger and sadness. The beast in me wanted to rip apart the men who'd done this to her with my bare hands. For so long, I'd kept him under control, but without her…

Without her, there'd be no point.

I reached out a hand to her lifeless body, needing to touch her, to feel her, at least once, but the chains now encircling my wrists stopped me just short of her too-still body.

"Not so fast," Gideon said and I spit fire at the sight of his face, singeing the top of his hair.

I took pleasure in the sight of his hastily covered surprise and fear. I would enjoy ripping him apart limb from limb.

But then he dipped down and jerked Elena's body against his. His maniacal eyes tinged with pleasure at my outrage.

"Let her go," I hissed.

"I don't think so."

"Whatever you want," I told Gideon. "Don't hurt her."

"I already have what I want," he said. Then with one move, so quick I barely saw it, he drew the knife along her throat and a river of red began to spill down her front.

I fell to my knees, my howl of despair so loud it shook the trees. But it did nothing to stop the river of blood that poured from her wound. They'd bound my hands so I couldn't even use them to stop the bleeding—even though I knew it was useless. For a horrifying moment, I considered cauterizing the wound with my fire, but I wasn't sure if that would hurt her even more.

The moment of indecision cost me, and she bled out before I could do anything at all.

I was soaked in her blood. I moved as close as I could

to her lifeless body. Alaric made a sound behind me, but I had attention for no one but her.

Even Gideon ceased to exist in my mind.

For long minutes, I was swallowed by an abyss of grief.

She didn't wake up. My body understood before my mind could catch up. Before I recognized what I was doing, I stood and pivoted, bringing up one bloody claw to slash through the soot-stained air at the man who no longer held a claim to my mate. *My* Elena.

He wasn't her brother. He was barely even a man in my eyes. He was certainly less than human and didn't deserve an ounce of my compassion, despite what Elena may have thought.

Injured though I was, I reacted with an instinct borne of thousands of years of battle. Instinct that urged me to protect my mate at any cost, to avenge those who harmed her by any means necessary. It was otherworldly, the rage that fueled my revenge.

White-hot the fury rose inside me, obliterating all of the remaining humanity I'd clung to for so long. Without Elena, there was no reason to hold out hope any longer. Without her, there was no need to hold my murderous impulses in check. When it came down to it, there was no point in living without her. My thunderous snarl echoed off the walls of the castle, rattling the icicles pointing dangerously below, and causing the snowdrifts to explode in every direction.

As the fury overtook me, I remembered, barely, to keep the fight away from the castle. *The hatchlings.* They were the only thing I refused to destroy. I'd take every human and every capital soldier with me, but I'd not harm them. Even if they'd never take wing, I still believed they had a chance. It may be too late for me, but I still held out hope for them.

With that thought, I managed to shift, surprising the men who still held my chains. They cut into the spines of my wings and dug into my snout. Either they would break or I would—I was past caring.

But I knew, the same way I knew Elena was mine the moment I saw her, I wouldn't be the one breaking. In the end, they may take my life, but they would lose theirs if they dared.

I took sick pleasure from the look on Gideon's face when I took wing, my strong wingspan carrying me out of the human's reach. With one powerful breath, I dove for the nearest human, the one who'd held a knife to her throat, managing to snare his retreating body in my claws. He struggled, but I liked that he did. He stunk with fear and piss and shit and if I could have laughed in my dragon form, I would have. Because I couldn't, I did something much better. As he screamed, I took him into my mouth, my teeth crushing his delicate bones until his throat snapped and he stopped screaming. I spit him out like a spoiled bite of food.

I wasn't done.

The humans had started to scramble while I killed their friend, but they were no match for my anger. Alaric, I noted as I flew past, had rallied the castle guard and was slaughtering the remaining mortals with complicated spellwork, the runes on his hands glowing like stars.

"For Elena!" he shouted.

"For Elena!" they chorused.

Hearing her name brought a fresh wave of pain and I sped up until I was level with Gideon, who'd shifted to flee. I flapped one wing and knocked him to the ground with a satisfying thud. I half-shifted, retaining my scale-armor and claws. I didn't want to kill him like I had the first. I was going to use my bare hands and bathe in his blood.

They wanted a beast? They would get one.

Gideon rolled onto his back, his eyes white and wide with fear. I could scent it on the air, and it made the dragon inside me roar with satisfaction.

"Don't kill me," he pleaded. "I'll give you—I'll give you whatever you want."

"Good," I said, my voice more dragon than human. "Very good."

"M-money?" he stuttered. "Jewels, land. Whatever you want."

"I'll bet that's what you promised the humans to get them to attack us, to poison your sister. They're always greedy for whatever they can get their hands on. But," I said, leaning forward, "I'm not a human and the only thing I want is your life."

I lunged, grabbing his cloak and twisting as I rose to my feet. I released my wings and flew us back to the spot where Elena's body rested. He would see what he had done and it would haunt him as his life drained away...along with his blood.

Except...her body was gone.

I whirled, Gideon still held aloft in my grip, still struggling to free himself, but Elena was nowhere in sight.

"Alaric," I called, "find Elena."

Fear and fury collided. If one of those dirty, grubby handed bastards put one more hand on her, the entire country would pay for it. I wouldn't stop until their children and their children's children paid for what they'd done to her.

As Gideon pleaded with me, Alaric and the guards searched, having tied up the humans and thrown them in piles by the steps. But they couldn't find her either. My hold on Gideon relaxed enough that he could draw breaths through a purpling face.

I reached out, closing my eyes, ignoring all the chaos around me, and concentrated on the thread between my solar plexus and hers. Her being and mine. If there was enough life, even a little, remaining in her body, I hoped it would lead me to her so I could put her to rest. The thought was abhorrent, but I forced myself to push even harder. There was nothing.

"Rhys!" Alaric shouted, but I ignored him, trying to concentrate.

Then, I felt something. Something different. My heart thudded in my chest. Certain I was making it up, I turned back to Gideon to deal with him.

Then I'd seek vengeance.

"Rhys!"

But there was a tugging, nagging feeling I couldn't get rid of. I snarled and tossed Gideon's limp body on top of the other humans.

"Tie him up," I told Alaric. "I'll figure out what to do with him after I find Elena."

Alaric punched me, snapping my head to the right. Then he pointed to the sky. "LOOK!" he shouted in my ear.

Against the blackened sky and surrounded by stars, a brilliant light shot across the horizon. My heart stirred, my dragon hissed, and I scowled. I didn't have time for this.

I started to say as much, but then the light grew

closer and I realized it wasn't a light at all. It was a small dragon, but its scales were glowing and gold-slicked. It was like no dragon I'd ever seen before.

"What in the bloody hell is that?" Alaric said.

"A phoenix," Gideon whispered in awe, and I motioned for the guard tying him up to bind his mouth as well.

Phoenix.

I'd heard of phoenix shifters, though they were rare. There was only one in Acasia at any given time, but no one had seen one in decades. He couldn't be right.

"Rhys," Alaric said beside me.

I ignored him, my eyes locked on the soaring figure as it grew closer. No one had seen a phoenix in decades. Since Elena's mother had died bringing her into the world, I realized.

My feet automatically carried my body backward, and I wanted to flee, but Alaric, who was stronger than he looked, gripped a hold of my arm and held me in place.

The phoenix was slim, but powerful, and had a tail of multicolored feathers that trailed after it. It was the most beautiful shifter I had ever seen. My dragon rumbled its approval in my head and I reared back against Alaric's hold, not comprehending.

It landed in front of us, engulfed in blinding yellow light. When I managed to refocus I found a naked woman in its place. I fell to my knees at her feet, my head bowed.

Certain I was seeing things, but absolutely overjoyed by the delusion, I pressed my head into her stomach. My dirty hands rounded her hips, and I released the breath I'd been holding since I saw her die right in front of me.

"Elena," I breathed.

She tipped my chin up, and I drank in her blessedly unblemished features. "Rhys," she said with a sigh. Someone brought her a cloak to cover her body.

"I don't understand," I said, reaching out a hand to touch her face. "How is this possible?"

Her smile was radiant. "A phoenix can only be reborn after they die. I'm as surprised as you are."

"This isn't possible!" Gideon shouted. "You aren't supposed to be able to do this."

Elena turned to face her brother. The strange gold glow emanated from her skin. I was in awe of her, wrecked by losing her and getting her back. I wouldn't feel she was safe until I held her in my arms for a month at least. Maybe two. Maybe an eternity.

"You've been planning this since you sent me to the temple, haven't you? Maybe longer. Tell me, Brother. For once in your life, tell me the truth."

Gideon was beaten. If I were him, I'd run myself through with a sword and get it over with, but there was a greediness in his eyes. He'd never give up willingly. "It was never fair. I was the oldest. I trained with father my whole life until you were born. When you came, you even took mother away, but everyone still loved you because you were to be Queen. I knew I'd never get anything for myself unless I *took it.* So I started with Father."

Elena faltered at that, but I held her upright. "Father?" she repeated faintly.

"He would have tried to stop me. The sentimental old fool. The poison that would have killed you has been slowly killing him for years, too. If you would have taken it like you were supposed to the night of the dinner, none of this would have happened."

"You did all of this so you would be King?" The disbelief and pain was raw in her voice.

"I deserved it!" he shouted. "A phoenix. It should have been me."

Elena froze for a moment. I moved to put myself between them. Then she turned, her hand darting out with supernatural speed. Before I could stop her, she was thrusting a dagger into her brother's chest.

"*This* is what you deserve," she croaked out as his blood spurted over her hands.

When he was dead, she got to her feet, the dagger dropping to the ground. The too large cloak she wore dropped over one shoulder revealed her skin streaked with blood. Her glow had dimmed, but it shone from new eyes, which must have turned gold after her shift.

I'd never cared that she couldn't shift. I loved her as she was with no reservations. But when she came to me, her arms wrapping around me, I knew. I knew it down to my bones and the heart of my dragon's soul.

She was my true mate.

When she'd hugged me long enough, she pulled back. "You saved me," she said.

I shook my head. "No, I didn't. I'm sorry, Elena. I'll never be able to apologize enough."

She put a bloodied finger to my lips. "You did. It was our bond that kept me tethered to this world. I died, but your love brought me back. I didn't get to tell you this before, but I love you, Rhys. I love you, *so much*."

Smiling, I said, "I know."

"What? How do you know?"

It was Alaric who answered, "That." He pointed to the skies, where hundreds of dragons were soaring overhead.

"But what does that mean?" Elena asked.

"Your love broke the curse," I told her, then scooped her into my arms and took her inside.

EPILOGUE

ELENA

The war wasn't over, but we won the battle.

Trouble was coming for Acasia, but this time, we'd be prepared and we wouldn't be alone.

In the garden where Rhys had showed me the *mirror* of my father and roses bloomed eternal, I watched him crouched patiently beside a tow-headed little boy who could be his miniature. Goddess save me. They were practicing how to fly and I was trying not to intervene.

"He'll be alright," said a voice beside me.

I turned to my father and smiled. "That doesn't mean I won't worry about them," I answered.

Father wrapped an arm around my waist. My eyes closed and I soaked him in. Three years had passed since we brought him to the Northlands where we ruled

Aurelia and it's shifter kind, but I never forgot what it had been like when I thought I might lose him.

"You'd think with your abilities you wouldn't worry," Father said.

"You'd be wrong." My breath caught in my throat as Rhys and our son leapt into the air, joining dozes of other dragon shifters in the skies. The little set of wings beat furiously to keep his wriggling body aloft. "Just because I can heal him doesn't mean it doesn't hurt my heart to see him injured."

It had been years since my true form had been revealed, but I still wasn't used to my abilities. I hoped I never would be. Not being able to shift like other of my kind had given me a deep appreciation for my gifts. I soon learned that not only was I able to shift into the phoenix, but my touch also caused wounds to knit themselves back together and brought those inches from death back to life. It fit, considering healing brought me such joy during the darkest time in my life.

My first act once I discovered my powers had been to bring my father home to our castle in Fellenor. At one touch, I was able to extract the poisons Gideon gave him. With time, he was back to his old self and decided to stay with us in the Northlands.

"You never like to see your child harmed," Father said. I glanced at him, but his expression was upturned at my son and for once it wasn't clouded with regret.

For a while after he'd been told what Gideon did, Father shouldered the blame. He'd been convinced if he'd been a different kind of man, Gideon wouldn't have been so vengeful. The truth was, Gideon was responsible for his own actions and in the end he paid for them. We mourned the loved one we thought we knew and with time, we'd come to terms with his death.

It may make me an awful person, but I didn't have regrets about taking his life.

"*If you're an awful person, then so am I. We can be awful together,*" Rhys said through our blending of minds.

"*Because you're stuck with me,*" I answered.

"*Forever and ever.*"

When our son fell asleep in my arms later that evening, I brought him to his rooms and laid him gently in his bed. He was the little soul in the egg, the one who'd waited for us for so long. It was a miracle we never took for granted.

Rhys wrapped an arm around my my waist from behind and rested his head on my shoulder. "He's so angelic when he sleeps," he said.

"That's to make up for causing such trouble during the day. He gets that from you."

Rhys didn't argue. Our son didn't only look like him, he was as determined and charming as his father. He was also as mischievous.

"And he gets his strength and kindness from you," Rhys said.

"You're only being sweet because you like seeing me miserable."

Chuckling, Rhys caressed the swell where our second child was growing. "That I won't deny. You're beautiful when you're pregnant. My dragon can't get enough of you."

I smiled ruefully. "I'm aware. Thank the Goddess she should be here any day now."

"What makes you think it's a girl?" he asked.

"I just know."

Soon, little Kiran would have a baby sister. Her name would be Julianna, after my mother. She would join a multitude of new hatchlings being born every day since we broke the curse. Like her brother, she was already so loved.

I couldn't ask for anything more.

I sought out the familiar landscape of my mate's mind. Reality was so much better than I could have ever imagined.

"*I love you*," I told him. Just as I had every spare moment since our love drew me back to him.

That was our deal.

ACKNOWLEDGMENTS

Get ready, this is going to be long winded. Because I've been waiting for this moment for what feels like an eternity.

I finished *Deal with the Dragon* in 2015. Back then, it was known as BOUND. The idea came to me after scrolling through Pinterest, no doubt in the middle of the night, when I saw one of those writing prompts about a girl whose father had sold her to a dragon and he was coming to collect his prize—her.

The book poured out of me in the following months like no other before it. Which was strange, considering it was far outside my regular genre. At the time, I had just published the first few novels in the *First to Fight* series so it was all military romantic suspense, all the time. Perhaps that's why it's taken me so long to dust this manuscript off the shelf.

In part, I think it was because I was afraid to do this novel justice. The edits I received back were so amazing and so thorough I was overwhelmed by the sheer amount of work I would have to do. And let me tell you, this book was *work*. I printed the entire thing several times. Marked it up with color-coded glitter gel pens and post-its. I wrote pages and pages of notes expounding on the comments from my editor.

Then, I let it sit.

For years.

And years.

And years.

You see, back when I finished the book in 2015, designer Letitia from RBA Designs made the cover for the book. The first time I saw it, I cried. Now, I'm handy with Photoshop, if I do say so myself. I can whip up a cover or two, but there are times when the concept in my head simply doesn't translate to screen. I remember I was at a Chinese place waiting on food when I got the email for the mockups from Letitia. I screamed when I saw them, then I cried. She captured absolutely everything I wanted the cover to be and made it seem absolutely effortless. It was and is my favorite cover to date. I've been daydreaming for*ever* about holding this book in my hands.

I wanted the book to be worth of the phenomenal edits, the perfect cover, the incredible characters. And, let's be honest, maybe I was afraid I couldn't deliver.

But I guess that's part of publishing, part of creating, part of *living*. You have to let go at some point.

So this is me, thanking all the people who helped to bring this book to life and letting go.

Ashley Williams of AW Editing, who absolutely ripped this book apart. Your edits scared me silly because I knew they were what needed to be done to make this book shine like it deserved. I hated them for years because I didn't think I was capable of doing them right. I'm still not sure I did, but you were absolutely right about everything. Your work is impeccable and you make me a better writer. Even I take years to finish.

Letitia Hasser of RBA Designs, who brought my dream to life. I've waited so, so, so long to have this book in my hands. It's hard, writing these acknowledgments, to believe that it'll happen some day soon. Thank you so much for everything that you do. Your cover for this book…it sums up everything twelve-year-old me ever wanted to have when I dreamed of becoming an author.

Alana Albertson who has listened to me complain about this book for five years. Who has championed me to publish it for nearly as long. Who keeps me sane. Thank you.

Karen Hrdlicka of Barren Acres Editing, thank you for taking me on last minute (again). Thank you for taking a chance on a genre out of your norm.

To my eagle eyes Jayce Cruz, Ariel Mareroa and Stephanie Martens for pointing out typos. You are my superheroes.

Readers, who have waited…an embarrassingly long time for me to get my shit together and actually release this book. I hope it lives up to your expectations. I hope you love it as much as I do and even if you don't, I hope you think the cover is kickass. Thank you so very much for your support, encouragement, and faith. I couldn't do this day in and day out if it weren't for you.

Thank you.

Nicole Blanchard is the New York Times and USA Today bestselling author of dangerous romance from antiheroes to aliens. She and her family reside in the Sunshine State along with their menagerie of animals. Nicole is represented by Katie Monson at SBR Media.

Visit her website www.authornicoleblanchard.com for more information or to subscribe to her newsletter for updates on sales and new releases.

facebook.com/authornicoleblanchard

x.com/blanchardbooks

instagram.com/authornicoleblanchard

amazon.com/Nicole-Blanchard

bookbub.com/authors/nicole-blanchard

goodreads.com/nicole_blanchard

pinterest.com/blanchardbooks

tiktok.com/@authornicoleblanchard

threads.net/@authornicoleblanchard

An Immortal Fairy Tale Series

Deal with the Dragon

Vow to the Vampire

Kiss from the King

Standalone Novellas

Bear with Me

Darkest Desires

Mechanical Hearts